Olé!

Tess swept the comforter around her shoulders like a matador's cape, then with a skip, a giggle and a half turn, she fell onto the bed. The comforter moved across her, exposing a length of thigh, a hint of nipple, the seductive curve of her waist.

A grinning Asher dived for her just as she sat up to untangle her legs. He only had time to grunt in alarm before he slid across the satin sheets and rapped his forehead against the edge of the bedside table.

"Owww. Damn it!" He flopped onto his back, one hand on his forehead, his eyes shut tightly.

"Oh, Ash," Tess moaned. "Are you okay, love?"

"Love?" He opened his eyes. "Say that again and I'll be good as new. Better than new."

"Love," she said, letting the *l* roll off her tongue. Then she forced his hand away from his forehead and kissed the red spot underneath. "Poor, darling Asher. If I'd known you were going to tackle me, I wouldn't have moved an inch. . . ."

Delayne Camp drew on her background as a newspaper journalist to write *A Newsworthy Affair*. She majored in journalism at the University of Tulsa and worked as a reporter before turning her talents to romance seven years ago. "There's a lot of me in this heroine," Delayne says, and admits that her witty character was a lot of fun to be with. She hopes that readers will enjoy Tess and Asher as much as she did.

Though *A Newsworthy Affair* is Delayne's first Temptation, fans of this award-winning author will recognize her particular brand of sophisticated humor. Delayne has published under various pen names, including Deborah Camp, Elaine Camp, Elaine Tucker and Deborah Benet.

A Newsworthy Affair
DELAYNE CAMP

Harlequin Books

TORONTO • NEW YORK • LONDON
AMSTERDAM • PARIS • SYDNEY • HAMBURG
STOCKHOLM • ATHENS • TOKYO • MILAN

Published March 1990

ISBN 0-373-25389-3

1

"WELL, IF IT ISN'T Moxie Maxie!"

Tess Maxwell stiffened and her fingers convulsed on the newspaper she held. She was glad she had her back to the man who'd just spoken, so that he couldn't see her initial expression of panic. *Get hold of yourself*, she commanded. *You're not a flighty, lovesick campus cutie anymore!*

Fixing a haughty smile on her lips, she spun around to confront her college nemesis.

"Hello, Asher," she purred, arching a brow as she noted his impeccable gray pin-striped suit, blindingly white dress shirt, the tie bearing stripes of gray, black and ocher. "I see you're following me again. I can't seem to shake you." She shook her head at the dilemma. "Kind of like a recurring nightmare."

His silvery-gray eyes drifted down over her lilac shirtwaist dress and came to rest on the newspaper she had folded into thirds. "Checking out the competition or merely exercising good taste?"

Wishing her timing wasn't so rotten, Tess tucked the newspaper under her arm in what she hoped was a nonchalant gesture. "I always get a copy of the morning paper to see what news was missed or inadequately reported."

Asher Ames chuckled warmly and stepped up to the newsstand in the lobby of the downtown hotel. "I'm glad to see the years haven't dulled your sharp wit, Tess." He bought a racing form and a copy of *The New York Times*. "How long has it been?"

"Not long enough," she said.

"Six years, isn't it?" he asked, ignoring her caustic comment. "And here we are in the same ballpark again." He inched back his chin to give her another once-over. "Looking good, Maxwell. *Very* good. You're still unattached, right?"

"As if you're interested," she scoffed.

"Maybe I am." He lifted his black brows in sudden speculation. "What are you doing for dinner tonight? How about showing a stranger the town? I moved into my apartment last week and I haven't had a chance to look around much. I hear there are some good jazz places in Kansas City. Are the Royals playing tonight? I'm chomping at the bit to see them. You're still crazy about baseball, right?"

"How did you know I like baseball?"

"Dana told me."

"Oh. Dana." Tess started for the revolving door, her head full of memories. Dana, her college roommate, had gone steady with Asher for a few months, forcing Tess to listen to how clever and wonderful and fun he was—as if Tess didn't know. And then after the inevitable breakup, how cruel and lousy and heartless he was, which had caused Tess to breathe a sigh of relief that soon she wouldn't have to hear Asher's name fifty times a day. "Have you seen her lately?" she asked.

"No, not for years. I heard she's married and lives in Dallas."

"As usual, your sources are about as reliable as the weather. Dana's living in Joplin. I'd love to continue this *fascinating* conversation, but I simply must run." She flashed a fake smile and quickened her pace, but Asher pursued with characteristic perseverance.

"What about dinner tonight?"

"No can do. It's not good form to fraternize with the enemy."

"The enemy?" He shot out a hand, grabbed her elbow and brought her to a jarring halt. "Is that how you think of me?"

She started to tell him she thought he was better looking now than he had been in college, but wisdom prevailed and curbed her tongue. Still, she recalled he'd been voted one of the top ten sexiest men on campus in his senior year. He was twenty-eight now, holding his fighting weight, but growing prematurely gray. His once coal-black hair was shot through with silver. The effect didn't lessen his attractiveness, but added to it. Even when he'd been named editor of the college newspaper, a job she'd wanted herself, she'd been hard-pressed to resent him. There was something about him, she mused. Something powerfully male that reached out and aroused her femininity.

"Come on, Maxwell," he said in a velvety whisper as he plucked at her filmy sleeve. "We're not enemies. We're friends. Good friends."

"Since when?" she asked, inching away from him as alarm bells sounded in her head and resounded in her heart. "You were Dana's friend, not mine."

"It's not too late. Dinner. How about it? I'm willing to pay. I'll put it on the newspaper account and call it a business expense."

"Oh, that's swell of you, Ash." She rolled her eyes, but felt a smile in her heart. "You're impossible, you know." Examining his comically hopeful expression, she sighed and waved a hand. "Oh, what the hell. Okay. I'll meet you at the KC Strip for drinks. Do you know where that is?"

"Yes. Near Crown Center, right?"

"You've got it. I'll be there at seven."

"So will I. You've made me a very happy man."

"And you've made me late for my next interview," she said, stepping into the first available space in the revolving door.

"Anyone interesting?" he asked, clearly fishing.

Tess laughed knowingly. "You can read all about it this afternoon, Ash. Just like everyone else in Kansas City."

Asher stepped outside to watch the flash of her long, silky legs beneath her form-fitting skirt. He gave a little shake of his head, appreciating her rounded figure. More women should be put together like that, he thought, admiring the swell of her hips and the nip of her waist. Her blond hair was attractively streaked and fell just below her shoulder blades. The coloring was perfect for her olive-green eyes.

A voice at his back intruded on his thoughts. "Ames?"

Asher turned to shake hands with his new boss. "Why, if it isn't the managing editor of Kansas City's best newspaper," he joked, then grew more serious. "Good to see you, Harry."

"Am I late or are you early?"

"Both. I was early and you're late." He shrugged off the issue of time. "But the hotel restaurant is still open and serving up breakfast, so why worry?"

"Was that Tess Maxwell just leaving?"

"Uh-oh. Caught me flirting with the competition." He grimaced and motioned for Harry Caper to tackle the revolving door first. Grinning as he watched the portly man squeeze into the wedge of open space, Asher followed him into the hotel lobby. "Tess and I go back to college. In fact, I dated her roommate."

"Why didn't you date Tess?" Harry asked, his pursed lips causing his salt-and-pepper mustache to twitch.

"Good question. I always had the feeling Tess didn't approve of me somehow." He led the way to a white-draped table in the corner of the restaurant. "I have to tell you, Harry, I'm nervous this morning. First day on the job and all."

"Your butterflies won't last," Harry assured him. "Our staff is a friendly bunch. Before you know it, you'll be family." He glanced up at the waiter who'd stopped at their table. "I don't need a menu. I'll have a poached egg, toast and coffee."

"On a diet?" Asher asked with a sympathetic smile.

"Always," Harry said, groaning. "Your day will come, Ames."

"Don't I know it. By the time I reach thirty, I'll be fighting a spare tire, I'm certain. But until that time—" He winked at Harry. "Croissant with lots of butter, coffee and a glass of milk, please."

"You dog," Harry said, lifting his mustachioed upper lip in a snarl. When the waiter moved away, Harry settled back in his chair and loosened his tie. "What was Tess doing?"

"Buying our newspaper." Asher looked around at the busy restaurant. "Is this a favorite hangout for the press?"

"Yes, especially in the mornings. Being only a couple of blocks from either newspaper makes it handy. So, you knew Tess in college, eh? She's a firecracker, that one."

"She wasn't too hot around me. In fact, she was downright *polar*. I guess she's still smarting from my beating her out of the editor's job on the college newspaper." He fell silent as his mind filled with seven-year-old memories. "That's the only thing I can think of, but I never thought she'd hold a grudge for so long."

Harry ran a finger along the inside of his shirt collar and looked decidedly uncomfortable. "Maybe she's out of sorts because she's been run over by the same truck again."

"How's that?" Asher examined Harry's expression and a strong hunch socked him in the stomach. "Harry, tell me that Tess didn't apply for my job."

"Wish I could, my man." Harry's round shoulders rose and fell in a helpless gesture.

"But *why*? She's already entertainment editor, right? Why did she want to switch newspapers?"

"Because ours has a bigger circulation and our entertainment section is larger. You get three pages daily to her one. Sundays belong to you because the competition doesn't publish on Sundays."

"She wasn't seriously in the running, was she?"

"Until your application came in, she was leading the pack."

"That's *not* what I wanted to hear." Asher ran a hand through his hair and reviewed his earlier meeting with Tess. Poor kid. No wonder her greeting had been as warm as an arctic blast.

The waiter brought their breakfasts, giving Asher a few minutes to assess the situation and decide whether or not it was something he should worry about.

"You know, back in college I figured Tess would stay on the newspaper, but she didn't. Wouldn't even report for it anymore. I'd been planning to make her assistant editor, but she never stepped into the newspaper office again."

"So, she's a sore loser," Harry said, diving into his breakfast with zeal.

"Well, no . . ." Asher surrendered to his second thought. "Well, I guess she is, at that. She's competitive, that's for sure. When she goes after something, she puts her heart and soul on the line. I guess that's why when she falls, she falls hard. She gets shattered and can't pick up the pieces as easily as some of us, I suppose."

"You're making excuses for her," Harry noted.

"No, I'm—" Asher lifted one brow in concession. "Yes, I guess I am. I'm feeling lousy for having stolen another job from her."

"You didn't steal the job," Harry corrected. "You were hired because you're the best applicant. Tess is good. Very good. But you've got more experience in covering all kinds of entertainment and supervising a staff. Tess has been with the same newspaper since graduation." He waved his fork, dismissing the subject. "We were looking for scope."

"But you were going to hire her before I applied," Asher reminded him.

"That's right. But you *did* apply, so the case is closed. I'm glad to have you on board."

"You didn't want to hire Tess?"

"No, it's not like that at all. I like her. What's not to like? She's hardworking, ambitious, talented and personable."

"But?"

"She doesn't have the experience you have," Harry repeated, then winced as if he hated to say what was weighing on his mind. "And the truth of the matter is...." He paused, his eyes suddenly sharp and piercing. "Not a word of this to anyone. Understand?"

"Yes. Sure." Asher leaned forward, snared by curiosity. "What is it?"

"Well, the old man . . . our illustrious executive editor—"

"Ben Albright," Asher supplied.

"Yes, old Ben." Harry shook his head. "He's got some old-fashioned ideas. When it's between a man or a woman, old Ben always goes with the man. He says men are easier to work with." Harry shrugged. "I don't necessarily agree, but I'm not the executive editor. Ben is."

Asher released his breath between clenched teeth and looked aside until his flaring temper subsided. "I hate to hear that, Harry. Men like Ben Albright shouldn't get away with such prejudicial decisions. It's not only despicable, it's ignorant." He pushed aside the remainder of his croissant, his appetite gone.

"I agree, but there you have it." Harry sighed his regret. "I hope this doesn't make you regret joining our ranks."

"No, but it doesn't endear me to Ben Albright, either." Asher flicked back his cuff to check the time. "We'd better go. I don't want to be late my first day on the job." He picked up the check before Harry could. "My treat this time."

"You're not going to finish your croissant?" Harry asked, gazing upon it with greed.

"No," Asher said, dropping his linen napkin over the plate. "And neither are you, Harry," he added, laughing at Harry Caper's woebegone expression.

"I'M NOT GOING TO MAKE YOU GUESS who I'm having dinner with tonight, because you wouldn't guess right if I gave you a million chances," Tess said, draping her legs over the arm of the easy chair in her living room. She smiled as Dana Givens's sigh reached across the telephone lines from Joplin to Kansas City.

"Okay, so I'm waiting."

"Hold on to your hat," Tess ordered. "Ready? Does the name Asher Ames strike a familiar note?"

"Arghh!"

Tess released a peal of laughter, imagining her friend strangling herself. "Control yourself, Dana. There's more."

"More?" Dana croaked. "What can be worse than you going out to dinner with my ex-flame?"

"He got the job I was trying for," Tess said. "I've known about it for a couple of weeks, but I couldn't bring myself to tell you until now. Asher is the entertainment editor for the morning paper. He's my competitor."

"What have we done to be served such a huge slice of injustice?" Dana demanded. "I mean, we're both nice women. Why are we being haunted by the likes of Asher Ames?"

"Oh, he's not so bad. I've met worse. Lots worse."

"What's with you? He took that job away from you!"

"I know, but another part of me is saying that Asher couldn't take something that was never really mine. I don't know that I would have gotten that job even if he hadn't been in the picture." She closed her eyes, war-

ring with her injured pride. "What makes it almost un-
bearable is that this is the *second* time he's gotten a job
that I've had my heart set on."

"Poor thing," Dana crooned. "Asher's such a beast.
Why in the world are you going out with him? Isn't it
enough that you have to see him through business from
time to time?"

"I don't know why I agreed to this dinner date," Tess
confessed. "I had every intention of telling him to take
one giant step backward off the nearest bridge, but I
heard myself agreeing on a time and a place. Weird, isn't
it?"

"No, not where Asher is concerned. Listen, pilgrim,
and listen good," Dana said in a game imitation of the
Duke. "Asher Ames isn't just *any* man. He's got the
charm of a devil and the sex appeal of a movie star, but
mind my words of warning. Asher Ames thinks of
women as disposable toys. You got that, Tess?"

"Dana, please," Tess said, frowning at the receiver.
"That's not how I remember Asher. He was never a
callous playboy. But that's neither here nor there. I'm
not interested in him romantically." Even as she swore
it, something corkscrewed in her heart. "He's the competition, pure and simple. I'd be nuts to get personally
involved with him. It would be professional suicide,
and I haven't worked long and hard just to cut my own
throat."

"Who are you trying to convince?" Dana said with
sharp insight. "I hope you can remember that when he

delivers one of his megawatt smiles and looks at you as if you're the only woman in the whole wide world."

"Dana, give me some credit, will you?" Tess swung her legs around and stood up to stretch. "I've got to run. I'm meeting him at seven."

"You never did tell me why you're meeting him," Dana reminded her.

"Oh, right." Tess considered her answer carefully. "I guess I just felt sorry for him. He's new in town and all."

"Listen to yourself," Dana said with a disparaging laugh. "He's already working his spell on you, and you don't even know it."

"Oh, stop it. I just thought I'd tell you about seeing him because it's good for a laugh. I never thought you'd take it all so seriously."

"Does he know you were after the same job?"

"I'm sure he doesn't. I haven't told him about it and don't intend to."

"How does he look? Has he changed?"

"Not much. Just his hair. He's getting gray, but it looks great on him."

"I daresay a plaid leisure suit would look great on him," Dana said with droll humor. "*Be careful*, Tess. That man is positively treacherous."

"Right, right," Tess said, laughing under her breath. "Take care, Dana, and I'll talk to you again soon."

"'Bye, Tess. Thanks for calling."

Tess replaced the receiver and shook her head at her friend's dramatic concern. "Nut case," she said fondly. But Dana never did have a grip on things where Asher

Ames was concerned, she recalled clearly. Then again, neither had she. Maybe Dana was right. There was something about Asher. . . . *Oh, stop!* she told herself. *Now who's being nutty?*

She hurried from her apartment, located only a mile from Worlds of Fun amusement complex, one of Kansas City's tourist attractions. Driving toward the downtown area, she fretted that she might have dressed up too much for him. Heaven forbid, he might get the idea that she wanted to impress him! His ego was big enough as it was without her adding to it. Then she reconsidered and decided that she looked fine. Not too casual. Not too dressy. Her selection of tangerine silk shirt and black slacks with black pumps was perfect. She'd fashioned two small braids from the hair framing her face and brought them up and around to the back of her head where they were held by a black grosgrain ribbon. It was a style she liked because it kept her hair out of her eyes while leaving it full and untethered to fall over her shoulders.

Her hair was a honey color, but she'd allowed her beautician to highlight it last month and she liked the results. Subtle streaks of light to dark blond shimmered through it.

Finding a parking place near the door of the KC Strip, Tess checked her image in the rearview mirror before leaving the car and entering the bar of the crowded supper club. Asher had arrived before her and had commandeered a table for two near the center of the room. He stood and motioned for her to join him, looking dashingly off duty in navy-blue trousers and a matching lightweight sweater.

"Tess, Tess, Tess," Asher said, taking her hands and holding them out from her body as he filled his eyes with her.

"Asher, Asher, Asher," she mocked, laughing off his loss for words. She saw that he'd already ordered a drink for himself. "How long have you been here?"

"Not too long. Here, sit down." He held out the chair for her before pulling his chair around to sit beside her. He motioned for a waitress. "What will you have to drink, Tess?"

"A White Russian, please," she said, and the waitress nodded and veered back to the bar.

"You like 'em sweet, do you?"

"That's right," she said, eyeing his Scotch. "And you like 'em straight."

"That's me. Straight as an arrow."

"Right," she said, drawing the word out to two syllables. "I spoke with Dana earlier. She warned me about you."

A frown lined his forehead and tightened his mouth. "She doesn't really know me, so I wouldn't take what she had to say too seriously."

"I'm not taking *anything* too seriously tonight, so don't worry." She smiled at the waitress, who set a frosted glass in front of her. "Thanks." Tess tasted the drink, which was really an X-rated milk shake, then turned her attention back to Asher. "So how was your first day on the job?"

"Great. People are friendly here."

"Let's see...you were working out of Chicago, right?"

"That's right."

"Kansas City must seem dull after Chicago."

"No, not at all. I like Kansas City. Don't you?"

"Sure do. It's my kind of town. I've never wanted to leave it." She ran a forefinger around the rim of the glass, sensing that the action had captured his gaze. "But you've lived in several places since college. You're a little short on staying power. How long do you think you'll be in KC before your feet get itchy again?"

"As a matter of fact, I hope to stay around here for a long time," he said, flashing her a gleaming grin. "I've been looking for a job like this ever since I graduated from college. I'm glad to have finally landed it."

Tess took another sip of the drink and hoped her face hadn't revealed her displeasure at hearing that he was dug in.

"I met my right arm today. Do you know Skip Bailey?"

"Yes, I've met him." She refrained from adding that she also thought that Asher would be better off with a two-by-four as a right arm. "What was your first impression of him?"

"That he's young."

"Twenty years young, to be exact. He lacks a semester of credits before he gets a degree."

"Yes, I was surprised by that," Asher said, then paused to finish his drink. He set it down with a thump and furrowed his brow. "I guess it's okay though. He'll only be covering television for the most part."

Irritation raced down Tess's spine, making her sit up straight. "What does that mean? Do you think just anybody can cover and review the regular television season?"

"No, not just anybody," he amended, and Tess relaxed. "But it certainly doesn't require the expertise that films or live theater do."

His lack of vision slayed her. She looked away, staring blindly toward the restaurant area, the source of music and quiet chatter that infiltrated the bar. She'd been fighting this particular battle ever since she'd joined the newspaper staff, and it galled her to realize that Asher was as shortsighted as everyone else. But maybe that would work to her advantage, she thought. If she treated television with the same regard as she treated the other forms of entertainment she covered, she might draw readers away from the morning paper and into her ranks.

"What did I say to make you frown so?" he asked, one hand closing upon hers.

His touch rattled her; it took everything in her to keep from snatching her hand away. His fingers tightened slightly, and she realized she was staring at his hand resting atop hers. Looking up, her gaze collided with his. A knowing glint floated in the silvery depths.

"That's better," he said in a voice as smooth as the Scotch he'd been drinking. "I certainly don't want to displease you . . . in any way."

She let her gaze drift over his thick hair, parted neatly on one side and curling at his white collar. She had a feeling that his hair would be soft and silky to the touch. And his lashes...so black and plentiful. And his eyes...so intensely appealing. And his mouth...so wide and inviting. Desire unfurled in the pit of her stomach and rose up through her like a curl of smoke, finally reaching her heart, urging it into a quicker pace and warming her blood. Tess caught her breath and jerked her hand from Asher's. She released a low self-mocking laugh and shook her finger at his puzzled expression.

"You *are* treacherous. Just like Dana said. We were talking about business, so how did we get from that to holding hands?"

"It's easy. Let me show you—"

"No!" She removed her hands from his grasp and laughed with him, liking the sound of his low-pitched laughter. "Back to business...."

"I didn't invite you to dinner to discuss business," he said, waving aside the waitress as she approached.

"Why did you invite me?"

"Because we're old friends."

"We're not old and we were never friends," she corrected, looking around when he rose from the chair. "Where are you going?"

"Into the restaurant. I'm starved."

He guided her from the crowded bar into the less crowded restaurant, where they were shown to a table and given leather-bound menus. Steaks were the specialty and they ordered KC strips for two. That done,

Asher crossed his arms on the table and angled closer to her.

"Now what's this stuff about us never being friends?" He grinned and gave her a cagey wink. "You thought that one sailed past me, didn't you? Well, Robin Hood, your arrow found my heart. It pains me to think you never counted yourself as a friend of mine."

"Please, Ames," she begged with a roll of her eyes. "Save it for the socially naive. You know good and well that Dana was my friend and your friend and that's as close to friendship as you and I ever came."

"Okay. Would you buy 'close acquaintances'?"

"How about ships passing in the night," she ventured, earning another laugh from him that spiced her senses. "So, enough of this hyperbole." She smiled cunningly when his brows shot up at the ten dollar word. "Why *did* you ask me out to dinner? And don't hand me that stuff about you being a stranger in town. Men like you don't stay strangers long."

"Well, aside from being impressed by your vocabulary—" He chuckled at her narrowed glare, then grew chillingly serious as he captured her gaze and held it. "Would you believe that I asked you to dinner because you've never failed to make my blood run hot? You bring out the hunter in me, Maxie. You always have."

She was uncommonly warm. Perspiring even! Tess heard herself laugh, a high, fluttering trill that didn't sound like her at all. She felt her lips curve into a smile that felt phony. She knew that her face had taken on a red hue and her breathing had grown shallow. But what she was mostly aware of was the pulsing of her feminine self. If he was the hunter, then she was the hunted, and she felt it within the core of her. What's more, she liked it.

The waiter intruded on the tense, silent scene, and Tess wanted to throw her arms around the poor man in gratitude for sparing her from having to respond to Asher's bold statement. After he arranged the platters of juicy steaks and luscious trimmings on the table, Tess exchanged one ravenous appetite for another.

2

"THAT WAS THE BEST!" Asher's voice rose, crested and broke with excitement. "I haven't heard jazz played like that since the last time I was in New Orleans."

"I told you this was a special place," Tess said, tucking her hand into the crook of his arm as they made their way from the nightclub to Asher's car.

"Why did you want to leave? It's still early."

"Yes, but this isn't the best part of town," she explained. "After midnight this place gets unruly, and it's past eleven now. Besides, I'm dead on my feet."

"I don't believe it. I remember when you'd work all night on the newspaper and then go directly to class without even paying a visit to your dorm room. You've always had incredible energy."

"That was seven years and too many all-nighters ago." She stood beside his car, shifting from one foot to the other while he searched for his keys. The night had grown colder, the wind stronger. She wished she'd worn a scarf and gloves. When Asher began a second trip from one pocket to another, Tess bent forward to peer through the smoked glass into the dusky car interior. Metal glinted, dangled, teased. "Don't bother, Asher," she said, sighing heavily. "Your keys aren't out here in the cold with us. They're in there, all locked up nice and safe."

"Oh, no," he groaned, and slumped against the side of the car. He hammered its roof in frustration and looked around at the empty street. "Now what?"

Tess thought wistfully of the car keys in her purse and her own car parked in the KC Strip parking lot. She'd almost suggested that she and Asher take both cars to the nightclub, but she'd wanted to ride in his shiny fire-engine-red sports car. Scrutinizing the car door and its lock, she surmised that a coat hanger wouldn't do. There was nothing to hook. The latch and lock were tucked under the protruding armrest to discourage amateur thieves.

"I guess we call a cab," she said.

"And leave my car here?"

"Do you have an extra set of keys?"

"Yes, back at my place."

"We'll take a cab back to the restaurant, get my car, go to your apartment, get your keys, come back here, open your car and then say goodbye and good riddance to each other," she said, counting off each step of the procedure on her cold, quivering fingers. "So, let's go call a cab."

"I can't get into my apartment, because my door key is locked inside my car," he explained, denting her perfect plan.

"Oh." She considered the dent. "Okay. We'll get your apartment manager to open up."

"Right." He smiled grimly. "That should work. I'll go call for a cab. Be right back."

"Oh, no." She shook her head and started for the club. "I'm not staying out here by myself."

She trudged beside him to the club and inside where it was warm and noisy. Asher had to shout into the phone receiver to be heard, but he finally made the dispatcher understand his location.

"Let's wait inside out of the wind," Asher suggested, taking his post at the door where a circle of glass afforded a stingy view of the dark, deserted street. After a few moments, he looked at her with sad eyes. "I'm sorry about this. I've never locked my keys in the car before. I don't know... I guess I was so involved in hearing the jazz band and being with you—"

"Don't blame me for this," she said, smiling.

"No, that's not what—"

"And don't be so serious," she chided, placing a hand on his arm and giving it a squeeze. "It's no biggie."

"You can go on home, you know. There's no reason for you to traipse back to my place. I'll just call another cab to bring me back here once I have my spare keys."

"And miss all the excitement?" she teased, knowing she should call it a night and let him handle this minor dilemma. But she found she didn't want to leave him in the lurch. It was obvious that he appreciated her company, and she was flattered.

The sound of a crash, followed by the tinkling of glass, brought her gaze sharply to his.

"What was that?" Asher asked.

"I don't know. . . ." Tess pushed open the door and looked down the street toward Asher's car. Three men in leather jackets and chains stood around it. One was reaching through the window he'd just smashed with a hand-held wrecking ball.

"Hey! You guys get away from there!" Tess dashed out, waving her fists, and started running toward the car. "What's the big idea? You're nothing but a bunch of thieving Neanderthals!"

"Tess, for crying out loud!" Asher reached out, gripped her arm and forced her to check her charge. He pushed her behind him and strode forward with purpose. The robbers had already begun making a retreat and now broke into an all-out run, the sound of their footsteps bouncing off walls of brick and mortar. Asher stopped by the driver's side and examined the smashed window. He stuck his hand in and wrested the keys from the ignition. Dangling them like a bauble in front of a jewel thief, he grinned. "Problem solved. Nice of those guys to save us the trouble, wasn't it?"

Struck by the absurdity of it, Tess laughed, then laughed more when she saw a taxi turn the corner and cruise toward them. She pointed, unable to speak, and Asher spun around and chuckled. He waved down the cab and spoke to the driver briefly. The taxi roared off into the night.

"Do you mind opening my side?" Tess asked, stamping her numb feet. "I'm freezing."

He unlocked his door, hit the automatic door lock and opened hers. Tess slid into the bucket seat, glad the ordeal was over and she was on her way home. He used his handkerchief to sweep glass particles from the driver's seat before folding himself into the car. Asher's chuckle went a long way toward warming her up, and she glanced at him, curious about his sense of humor. He started the car and adjusted the heating vents.

"It's all or nothing with you, isn't it?" he asked as the car purred like a big cat and the air coming from the vents began to chase away the chill. "I mean, you either charge or retreat. It never occurs to you to stand still and assess the situation. Those guys could have attacked you." He released a bark of laughter. "Hell, didn't you see the ball and chain dangling from that guy's hand?"

She considered his words and realized he was right. "I guess I've seen *West Side Story* too many times," she admitted, laughing at her own rash action. "I do tend to act on gut instinct."

"Like during college when you quit the newspaper just because I was editor?"

"Noooo," she said slowly, her blood starting to simmer as it always did when she thought of that time. "I quit the newspaper because *I* wasn't editor."

"All or nothing," he said, putting the car into gear and sending it forward. "If you'd stayed on the newspaper I would have made you my assistant editor."

"A consolation prize?" She held up one hand to stop him before he could speak. "That's how I would have thought of it back then." She sighed, shaking her head at the foolish youngster she'd once been. "I resented you. I blamed you for being better than me."

"I wasn't better...."

"That's how I saw it. That's how it was." She made a face, disliking the conversation. "Why go over it now? It's history. Maybe I was wrong back then, but I was young and impulsive."

"And now you're older and impulsive," he concluded. "If you'd accepted the position, then you would have been a shoo-in for editor the next year, after I'd graduated. If you'd wanted the job that badly, you would have had it the next year."

"I wanted the job *that* year."

"Well, we don't always get what we want when we want it," he said, his glance as sharp as the wind rushing through the hole in the car window.

"You must have read that somewhere, because I know you've never experienced it personally," she said, turning her head so that he wouldn't see the pain in her eyes that belied her stony words.

"What do you know about me?" he challenged, then went on as if he knew she couldn't answer him. "You've been harboring resentment toward me all these years...."

"I have not! I haven't given you a thought. Not one thought!" Even as she made the assertion, she felt the lie in her heart. She *had* thought of him occasionally, but she'd long since stopped resenting him. Maturity had made her see that it wasn't Asher's fault he'd been chosen over her, but it didn't ease the disappointment all that much. Even now she felt the weight of disappointment in her mind and heart because he'd been given the job she'd felt had been hers. Life wasn't fair, she knew, but why did it have to be so ironic, so cruel at times?

Glancing sideways at him, she fought the urge to come clean and admit to him she'd followed his career through the grapevine. She'd told herself she was only mildly curious, but it had been more than that. She'd been curious about him, wondering if all the promise within him had been revealed, fulfilled. His talent had blinded her in college; it had glowed in the words he strung together like so many bright lights and colorful beads. She'd been surprised when he changed from writing hard news to softer features and then, lo and behold, film and play reviews! Just like her. Knowing he was on the same track was like feeling the bite of a whip, sending her racing faster and farther, trying to outdistance him. He wouldn't sprint past her again, she'd vowed.

But he had. She swallowed hard, feeling tears gathering in her throat and behind her eyes. She hadn't even see him coming before he'd sailed past to claim the prize again and leave her choking on his dust.

She wondered if he had ever thought of her. And what he had seen in her back in college, or whether he had seen her at all.

"Did you know I was living here?"

He furrowed his brow, confused for a moment, then he nodded as he caught on. "Not at first. I was interested in the job, so I nosed around before I applied. I looked at the competition and saw your byline."

"And?" she asked, wanting more.

"And I thought it would be fun working in the same town as you."

"Fun?" She made a derisive sound, then squared her shoulders. "Well, the battle lines are drawn."

"Battle lines?" He laughed at such a notion. "Get real. We're not mortal enemies." He rolled his eyes dramatically. "I swear, Maxwell, sometimes you make a pit bull look like a pussycat."

"Thanks," she said, resting on one hip so that she practically had her back to him. "I'll add that to my cache of compliments."

"Tess, I didn't mean—"

"The restaurant is up ahead. Don't miss the turnoff," she said, grateful they'd arrived. Should have listened to Dana, she thought. Going out with Asher Ames had been one giant mistake. He had an uncanny ability to keep her off balance, make her head spin and her heart race. "I guess you have insurance on your car," she said, looking for a safe, dull topic.

"Yes, I do."

"You should put something over the window tonight in case it blows up a rain."

"I'll do that." He stopped his car directly behind hers and turned sideways to face her. "Tess, I'm sorry our evening struck a bad note. I was having a great time before—"

"It's okay," she said, yanking on the door handle, then realized it was locked. She pushed the red lever, but before she could open the door, the lever slammed back into the "lock" position again. Startled, she looked toward Asher and his grin cleared up the mystery. "Asher, please unlock the door. I'm tired and I'm not in the mood—" The harsh, lush press of his mouth on hers stopped her words and her heart for a split second. Her head cleared and she sucked in a deep breath as her eyes widened and her mouth dropped open in outrage. "Oh, you! How...who...why...don't laugh at me!"

He kept laughing, head thrown back and body shaking with amusement. Tess gave him a pop on the shoulder, then unlocked the door again. Before she could scramble from the car, Asher's arm shot out, capturing her around her waist and hauling her flush against him.

"Asher, stop! This isn't funny!" She struggled, but only for a few moments, only until his hot mouth closed over hers and his body heat enveloped her. He warmed her right down to her toes and set fire to her protests, sending them up in smoke.

The tickle of his hair against her hands triggered an immediate reaction. Tess slipped her fingers up through his hair, combing the back of it with long strokes of her nails, admiring the silky, silvery delights. His hands moved down her back, pressing her shirt to her skin, then back up, pulling it from her waistband. His mouth slanted against hers, and he released a tortured sound as he held her head in his big hands and stroked her lips with his tongue until they tingled. Just as she was about to open up to him like a bud in the springtime, he set her away so quickly that Tess felt like a sapling swaying in the wind.

Tess stared at him, trying to understand what had happened and why he had retreated from her. He brushed his hair back from his forehead, and the tremor in his hand told her more than anything he could have said.

"Ash?" She cleared her throat of its huskiness. "You okay?"

"Do I look okay?" he snapped, then caught himself and smiled. "Sometimes the past just won't let go," he said in a whisper that held a yearning, heartrending nuance.

"I don't—" Tess shook her head, unable to decipher his meaning.

"It repeats itself, doubles the trouble, swindles you out of your future."

"What are you saying? You're talking in riddles."

His eyes were soft and his smile was full of regret. "I don't want to be your competition, Maxie."

"But you are." She sighed, feeling the burden of truth. "What's more, you always have been. Tonight didn't change that."

"No? Are you sure?"

"I'm sure that tomorrow I'll go to work and do everything in my power to scoop you, write better than you and steal readers from you." Pushing open the door, she didn't look back as she left his car for her own.

TWO DAYS LATER Tess was still thinking about Asher's kiss and the way his hand had trembled afterward and the yearning quality that had been in his voice.

She went through the motions at work, but at home she found herself drifting in a space somewhere between then and now. She daydreamed, and her nightly flights of fancy made her face sting with embarrassment in the mornings. Such erotic dreams! All of them starred Asher Ames.

Curled up in her favorite chair by the sliding door, a good novel open in her lap, Tess realized she'd read the same page ten times and didn't remember a word of it. Snapping the book closed, she pulled back the drape to let in the night. Strategically placed lawn lamps lit a pathway below her second-storey balcony. It was a moonless night, but not oppressively dark because of the star-pocked sky.

Giving up on the novel, she reached for a folder that contained office correspondence. Flipping through the contents of it, she found one large envelope from Century City and tore it open, knowing it would contain a business-related invitation. As she read the cover letter, she smiled. Oh, how she enjoyed the television junkets—those trips to California or Nevada to get advance viewings of the new crop of television shows, miniseries and movies and to interview the performers, directors and producers. Always good for mountains of copy, it was also great fun. Every television reporter looked forward to it and Tess was no exception. She lived for the twice-a-year blowouts.

She made a mental note to warn her boss it was coming up and the newspaper had damn well plan on paying her way! Tess rolled her eyes and stuffed the information back into the envelope, thinking of last year when she'd had to threaten to leave the newspaper before she was granted the travel expenses.

"We just can't justify the costs," Tess mimicked her managing editor. "It's so expensive to send you out there!"

The nerve of the man, she thought, recalling how she'd reminded him that every time a sports tournament was held anywhere in the country, he didn't think twice about sending out one of the sports reporters. She'd gotten her way, but what about this year? Would she have another battle on her hands? Another showdown? *Hope not*, she thought, letting her shoulders sag. She needed to save her strength for the competition.

Her gaze moved to the newspaper scattered across the couch. Leaving the rocker, she sat on the sports section and flipped through state and local news to the back pages saved for entertainment. It was Wednesday and Asher had been given three whole pages to her one. Well, actually her *half*—advertising had taken up the bottom of her sole entertainment page. She'd barely had enough room for her television guide grid and a severely edited obituary of a prominent film director. But Asher had white space up the whazoo day after day. It was disgusting.

She read his review of a new film, admiring his choice of verbs and his avoidance of adverbs, then she read an article about the deceased film director. It wasn't wire. She was certain of that. Asher's style was all over it. He'd researched the director's life, films and achievements, and he'd written a first-rate piece.

"You won't steal any readers from him this way," she said, throwing the section aside and burying her face in her hands, then scrubbing it harshly until her skin stung. "I'm doomed. How can I compete when he's got the bullets and I've got an empty gun?"

Tess bounded up from the couch and went to the glass door again, pulling back the drape just enough to look out. A sleek, low-slung car oozed in and out of view, and her heart soared into her throat. She let the drape fall back into place.

Asher! Asher was cruising the parking lot. Looking for an empty space? Oh, Lord! He was coming to visit!

She did a quick pass of the room. The scattered newspaper and leftovers of her burger, fries and large iced tea made her heart sink. Grabbing frantically at the mess, she stuffed the newspaper and food wrappers into a plastic trash can. Racing from couch to chair to rocker, she plumped up pillows, dusted tabletops with her shirtsleeve and hid the overflowing trash can in the closet. She plopped onto the couch, taking deep breaths and trying for a measure of calm before her doorbell buzzed and she'd have to decide whether to be at home or be out for the evening.

"Oh, did you come by last night?" she said, trying it on for size. "I was out . . . with a friend." She planted a knowing smile on her lips and quirked one brow just so. "Sorry I missed you. Perhaps you should call first next time."

She listened to a replay in her mind and decided it couldn't sound more phony if she said it with an English accent. Just open the door when he buzzes and ask him what brings him out on a night like this. She wondered if he was in the neighborhood or if he was thinking of her, then she decided he *must* be thinking of her to drive to her place unannounced. Why hadn't he called first? Was he afraid she might tell him not to come and then he'd be terribly disappointed? Tess giggled, finding the notion of a crestfallen, heartbroken Asher Ames positively hysterical. She'd answer the door and keep her mouth shut. Let him explain. She wouldn't open her mouth and stick her foot in it, thus giving him the advantage that he certainly didn't need because— She interrupted her own train of thought, checking her watch and straining her ears. What was keeping him?

Tess went to the sliding door again and peeked out. Nothing. No shiny car. No sound of a pampered engine.

"You're so dumb," she said, groaning at her own stupidity. He wasn't even out there. So, she'd seen a sports car. Big deal. Asher didn't have the market on sports cars cornered. She'd seen a car similar to his, and she'd jumped to the conclusion that he was just as preoccupied with her as she was with him. "Dumb, dumb,

dumb," she chanted, pulling the wastebasket out of the closet and giving it a swift kick. Papers spilled across the avocado carpet.

She didn't bother to pick up the mess, but dragged herself and her depression over to the stereo. Putting on an old, dearly loved album, she closed her eyes in relief as a husky, world-weary black woman's voice gave her self-esteem a motherly hug. Tess relaxed on the sofa, stretching out and flinging an arm over her eyes to block out everything but that wonderful voice.

The junket. Her mood lightened immediately at the thought. Ah, yes. It would be good to get away from this mess for a little while. Junkets were always good for a few laughs, three-course dinners, cocktail parties and endless entertainment and interviews. The soles of her feet tingled, making her wonder if she had a drop of gypsy blood in her veins. And she'd get to see her comrades again. There was a handful of guys she ran around with at those things, and she looked forward to catching up on their news, hearing them gripe about their jobs and malign their bosses. Misery loves company, she thought with a chuckle.

Yes, it would be good to get away from Kansas City and Asher Ames, she told herself, then grew rigid when she was struck by the flaw in her logic. Asher wouldn't be staying in Kansas City; he'd be at the junket right along with her!

Moaning and placing a pillow over her face, she rocked from side to side. The junket began to seem like a vacation in hell.

"I won't go," she mumbled into the pillow. "I just won't go. That'll make the boss happy."

But contemplating that alternative did nothing to relieve her aggravations. Damn it all, she wouldn't let Asher spoil her fun! She just wouldn't! She loved the junkets and, what was more important, they were a gold mine of articles and reviews for a good six months. Besides, he might not go, since he didn't care much for television reporting. Asher might send Boy Bailey in his place. She would wait and see. If Asher made reservations, she wouldn't. But if Skip Bailey's name was on the list of junket junkies, then she'd be on the next plane. Pulling the pillow away from her face, she frowned at the ceiling, ashamed of herself for being such a wienie. She wouldn't compromise her reporting just because Asher Ames was too hot to handle!

Speaking of handling . . . she wondered what Asher was doing tonight. Had he found a honey already? Was he wining and dining her? It was silly for her to have thought he'd be juvenile enough to drive through her parking lot without even stopping by to say howdy. That wasn't his style. But then, what did she know about his style except hearsay from Dana, who hadn't seen him in years. Maybe he would drive . . . No, he wouldn't . . . But he might have . . . *wait.*

She sat upright, speared by a recollection that made her eyes water. In her mind's eye she saw the sports car clearly, driving slowly past the apartment buildings, and the starlight playing over something that fluttered where the driver's window should have been. Something that could very well have been a sheet of plastic covering a hole in the window.

"It *was* him," she said, her fists coming up to rest against her leaping heart.

Seized with a burst of celestial joy, she jumped up from the couch and waltzed around the living room, edging around the coffee table and deftly dodging the rocker and stack of newspapers and magazines on the floor. The impromptu dance ended when she caught her reflection in the full-length mirror on the closet door. Tess stopped and stared at the flush-faced, bright-eyed, breathless young woman. She hadn't seen that woman since college, when the world had still been fresh and toasty and easy to digest. The recorded songster crooned in her ear, and Tess made the next two lines a duet.

"I've got it bad," she sang along, feeling the truth nestle, all comfy, in her heart. "And that ain't good."

3

SENSING THAT SOMEONE was hovering near his desk, Asher looked away from the computer screen to find his assistant, all toothy grin and freckles.

"What's up, Skip?" he asked, swiveling the chair around to face the cub reporter.

"What are you working on?"

"A story on the upcoming production of *Carmen*. What are *you* working on?"

"I just got a review tape on a PBS miniseries. Are we going to cover public broadcasting stuff?"

"Sure. Why wouldn't we?"

"Hardly any of it's made in America." He shrugged. "I got something else in the mail, too." He dropped the long folder onto Asher's desk. "It's an invitation to a major television junket. I suppose you'll want to go."

"I don't know. I'll take a look at it and let you know." He started to turn back to the computer, but paused when Bailey still hovered. "Something else?"

"Are you going to review that new movie this morning or do you want me to?"

"The new . . . oh, damn!" Asher bounded to his feet and flicked back his cuff to check the time. "I forgot all about it." He waved Bailey aside with one hand while he punched a key to save his copy on the computer with the other. "I'll go. Thanks for reminding me, Skip." He switched off the terminal and grabbed his suit jacket. "Be back after lunch."

Dodging desks and printers, Asher made his way through the newsroom and toward the bank of elevators. The elevator door closed out the din of teletype, ringing phones and rumbling voices that Asher barely heard anymore, having long ago become accustomed to the constant hum of activity. Slipping into his suit coat, he adjusted his tie and ran his hands along the sides of his hair in a rough combing.

Asher left the newspaper building and walked two blocks to the garage where he left his car during the day. The attendant waved, recognizing him and not needing to see Asher's claim ticket.

"Got that window fixed, I see," the attendant called across the rows of parked cars.

"Sure did. About time, right?" Asher said, his voice echoing through the garage. He unlocked the door, settled into the bucket seat and guided the car from the covered garage and out into the sunlight.

The dashboard clock told him he had ten minutes before show time. Good thing the theater was only five or six minutes away, Asher thought, relaxing a little. He tugged at his tie, giving his Adam's apple more freedom.

Usually Skip Bailey was about as useful as snow boots in Hawaii, but Bailey had earned his keep today by reminding him about the appointment. The film would open tomorrow, so Asher had to complete his review today to have it published in the morning edition. It was almost nine, he calculated, and the film would be over sometime around eleven. Man, oh, man, he'd have to move into high gear when he got back to the office; he had three other stories to finish.

He shrugged off the flutter of nerves in his stomach; it was all part of the job. Deadlines. Hurry, hurry, hurry. Getting the copy in right under the wire. Lucky for him he did his best work under pressure.

Asher parked his car behind the theater and entered through the fire door, propped open by the manager as Asher had requested. Pulling a narrow reporter's notebook from his jacket pocket and a pen from his shirt pocket, he moved on cat feet into the darkened theater. The young manager greeted him with a friendly nod.

Expecting a deserted theater, Asher hesitated when he saw a golden head near the front. Ah, the lovely, luscious Miss Maxwell! He was glad for the darkness when he couldn't keep the slaphappy grin off his face. Not having seen her since that weird dinner date almost two weeks ago, Asher had wrestled with a burning desire to make another date with her and the chilling knowledge that he was asking for trouble if he kept seeing her socially. He slowed his steps as the voice of reason told him to sit behind her and avoid any confrontation. She was trouble. Big trouble.

"I hate to trouble you, ma'am, but you're in my seat," Asher whispered, tapping a narrow shoulder encased in a jungle-patterned shirt. He chuckled when she turned wide green eyes on him. "But that's okay. I'll just sit next to you."

"Don't you dare!" She edged away from him, holding her notebook against her shirt as if it contained a secret code. "I don't want you cribbing my notes! Sit somewhere far, far away. Are you deaf?" she demanded when he sat two chairs from her. "That's not far, far away, Asher."

"Far enough. I can't read notes in the dark, Tess." He shifted more comfortably in the uncomfortable chair and frowned his disapproval. "Remember the old days when theaters had plush seats and carpet on the floors?" He lifted one shoe, then the other with effort. "Sticky," he said with a snarl. "Like they mop the floor with rubber cement." He devoured her with his hungry eyes. The lighted exit sign limned her profile with green. Her eyelashes seemed incredibly long against the strange light. And her skin! Flawless, soft, natural hues of copper, tan and peach. He remembered how it felt against his fingertips—smooth, warm satin. He smiled faintly at the way her nose tipped up right at the end and how her mouth, so lush and generous, was gathered into a piqued bud.

"I was curious about where you live, so I drove by your place the other night."

Her head snapped around so quickly that her hair fanned out and then settled around her shoulders in a shimmering mantle. She stared at him slack jawed, as if he'd just admitted he was a flasher. Her teeth clicked together decisively, and she turned toward the screen as images began to flicker across it.

Shaking his head at her overreaction to his innocent revelation, Asher flipped open his notebook and uncapped his pen. He focused his attention on the celluloid mystery, finding the woman beside him far more entertaining and a sight more puzzling.

HE'S ADMITTED IT!

Tess stared blindly at the film review filling the computer screen, then pressed a key, putting it on the disk and sending it downstairs to the composing room. She shook her head, allowing herself—finally—to dissect her staggering morning. Asher Ames had sat next to her and admitted that he'd cruised by her apartment building the other night. Ooo, that really burned her toast!

She scrubbed at her face with one hand, filled with annoyance at the man. She'd felt secure in being privy to one of his little secrets, smug to know something he didn't want her to know, but then he'd ruined it for her. That man! He was constantly taking things away from her. He couldn't leave well enough alone by allowing her to have a little dirt on him. No-o-o-o! He had to snatch it from her grasp before she'd had the chance to really gloat over it.

"All through?"

Tess spun around to her boss. Jess Arnault raised his bushy gray brows at her wide-eyed stare.

"Something wrong?"

"No." Tess laughed nervously as her gaze fell upon the folder from Century City, and she grabbed at the diversion. "Nothing that your signature on a junket voucher won't fix." She picked up the folder and tossed it to the edge of her desk. "It's midseason replacement time, Jess. The powers that be are holding court in Las Vegas this year. Isn't that swell?"

"Tess . . . Las Vegas? I don't know. That's a lot of money . . . Las Vegas?" Jess scratched at his white beard and refused to even glance at the folder.

"We're not going to put the gloves on again, are we?" Tess asked, sighing with weariness. "Jess, you know how important these junkets are to me! I can't cover television without previewing the new series and miniseries."

"So, you'll review the shows *after* they're on the air," Jess said with a characteristic who-really-cares-anyway shrug. "Where's the tragedy?"

"Jess, that would be tantamount to the city desk reporters writing stories about events only *after* they've been held. Is that how you want our readers to view the entertainment section? You want us to be known for printing all the news that's a week old?" She stood, pumped up with fury. "If that's what you want, then you don't want me. I'm a journalist not a historian."

"Please, please," Jess begged softly, holding up his hands and cringing from Tess's tirade. "Who said you couldn't go to Nevada?"

"I can go?"

"We'll see."

"When will we see?"

"Soon."

"How soon?"

Jess sighed and rounded his shoulders. "Tomorrow. Is that too late? Can you manage to wait less than twenty-four hours without packing your briefcase and storming out of here forever?" His gentle smile transformed her lion's heart into a lamb's.

"I'm sorry, Jess. I guess I flew off the handle... again." She sat in her chair and sighed. "Tomorrow will be fine. You're a sweetheart."

"And you're too excitable," he said, then shuffled back to his office.

Stuffing notes and press releases into her briefcase, Tess smiled like a contented cat. Jess was going to let her go. She knew it. What a relief! She wasn't in the mood for a Mexican standoff. She snapped her briefcase shut, then hitched her purse strap higher up on her shoulder before grabbing the case in one hand and a portable computer in the other. After a quick dinner, she planned to spend a couple of hours writing a story endorsing another rating, one that would distinguish adult films from pornographic movies. That ought to put Asher Ames on his ear!

She'd labored hard on her film review, anxious to outshine his prose and insight. At least she'd scooped him. Her review had run that afternoon while his wouldn't see the light of day until morning. Before leaving her cubicle, she glanced at her desk to make sure she hadn't left behind the videotape of a new miniseries. She intended to view it while she ate dinner. Just a normal evening for an entertainment editor, she thought with a wry smile. She wouldn't mind the workload if she didn't feel as if she were spinning her wheels so much of the time. It was becoming more and more frustrating to preview television shows, write insightful pieces about the industry and conduct interesting interviews with people in the business when she rarely had enough newspaper space to print them!

Checking the big clock mounted on a center post in the newsroom, Tess was surprised to see it was almost five o'clock. She usually knocked off around two, having worked from six or seven in the morning. Traffic would be fierce, she thought, knowing she'd be caught in the middle of rush hour on the freeways. She whirled, head down and lost in thought as she started to leave her little corner for the big, wide world, but the sight of a pair of highly polished dress shoes brought her up short. She looked up into Asher's smiling face.

Blinking rapidly and praying he was a mirage, she felt her mouth drop open. Why, she wondered angrily, was she always rubber jawed around him?

"What are you doing here?" she whispered, glancing around to see that only a few of the staff writers and editors were present to view the confrontation.

"I saw your car still parked in the lot across the street and I thought I'd see if you'd like to grab something to eat before you head home tonight."

"No, I don't!" She lowered her voice and angled close so that she couldn't be overheard by the others. "And

I don't appreciate you coming here like this. What are you trying to do, discredit me?"

"Discredit . . ." He stuffed his hands into his trouser pockets and shook his head with world-weariness. "Will you stop it? We're not in the position to exchange state secrets, you know." He inched closer, thrusting his face near hers. "We're reporting on entertainment, not espionage." He straightened, his smile back in place. "So, how about dinner? You pick the place. I'm easy."

She lifted a brow, consumed with a comeback that she edited down to two words. "I'll bet."

He laughed, joining in with the fun. "Right, spread it around, okay?"

"I'm not a matchmaker and I'm not going out to dinner. I've got mountains of work tonight, which I plan to do with a cheeseburger in one hand and a tall lemonade at the ready." Feeling eyes on her, she realized that a few co-workers were doing everything but taking notes. "Look, do me a favor and don't come here again. This is where I *work*." She pushed past him, no easy feat since he seemed to enjoy the brush of her body against him. "Excuse me," she ordered, and he gave way with a chuckle.

The elevator car was crowded and she had to suck in her breath as the door slid shut. Much to her annoyance, Asher had wedged in beside her. The trip from the seventh to the first floor had never seemed to take so long before. Every place that Asher's body pressed against hers burned like a branding iron. Just as the car bounced to a stop, Asher sniffed the air and released a long, masculine sigh of pleasure.

"Mmm, Tess. That's the kind of perfume that gives a man all kinds of ideas."

A few of the men around her laughed softly as Tess felt her face burn with bright color. She stormed out of the motorized sardine can as soon as the doors parted enough to let her slip through them. She was well on her way toward the brass-and-glass doors that led to the sidewalk when Asher caught up with her and grabbed her computer case, stopping her cold.

"Let go!" She wrenched it from his grasp, but his charming smile took some of the wind from her sails. "You are the most infuriating man, Asher Ames! What's your game? Are you out to humiliate me at every turn? Embarrass me whenever possible? Anger me at random? What? Tell me!"

He shrugged. "If this is a game, then it's cat and mouse. The only question is, who's the cat and who's the mouse? What do you think Tess? Care to venture a guess?"

"No." Her chest constricted, making it hard for her to breathe. "I've really got to—"

"I read your review. It was damned good, Maxie."

"Really?" She filled her lungs with sweet success. "I mean, you're not just saying that to soften me up, are you?"

"No, but if that's what it takes…" He shook his head, grinning at her flash of annoyance. "I'm kidding. Seriously, I enjoyed the review. I don't necessarily agree with it, but I enjoyed it."

"What don't you agree with?"

"You can read all about it tomorrow morning," he said, giving her a taste of her own medicine. "Gotcha!"

"Oh, you..." She glanced around and decided it was too risky to mutter such unladylike words in her place of business. "You can walk me to my car." She handed over the computer case. "Make yourself useful for a change."

He took the case good-naturedly and held open one of the heavy doors so that she could pass through ahead of him. Falling in step beside her, he leaned forward a little to catch her attention. "You know what you need, Tess Maxwell?"

"Why do I get the feeling your question is rhetorical and I'm not going to like your answer?"

"What you need is a good, old-fashioned love affair."

"Sure, sure," she said, rolling her eyes. "Will it clear up my complexion, too?"

"Your complexion is fine. Peaches and cream. What it *will* clear up is your disposition."

"My disposition is fine, too." Reaching her car, she turned to deliver a cool look and to retrieve her computer case. "If you don't like it, you don't have to hang around me. It's a free country."

"You work too hard," he said, setting the computer case down on the asphalt, then shielding it with his leg so that she couldn't reach it without difficulty. "And you don't play nearly enough. You were the same way in college. Work, work, work. Nose to the grindstone. It's a wonder I ever noticed you."

"This is all very entertaining, but—"

"But I *did* notice," he interrupted, taking a step forward so that she was forced to plaster herself against the side of her car. "And, although I think you could use a little loosening up, I'm glad I've run into you again."

"Good choice of words. I feel like a hit-and-run victim," she said, trying to make light of his dead-serious approach.

"I took notice the other night when I kissed you. Remember how shook up I was? It's because I was a hair's breadth away from taking you right then and there."

The tiny hairs at her nape quivered in reaction to Asher's feral smile.

"Since then I've had you a dozen times in a dozen different ways in my dreams," he whispered. "But I've got a craving for the real thing."

She placed a hand against his shirtfront, felt the beating of his heart and swayed toward that primitive tattoo.

He kissed her fully, his lips sliding over hers, his tongue testing the seam of her mouth then breaking through it to flirt with her tongue, tip to sensitive tip. Tess was about to close her eyes on the rest of the world when, in her peripheral vision, she caught sight of the parking attendant's face. She pushed Asher away, feeling her cheeks flame with embarrassment.

"What's gotten into me?" she whispered, shaking her head and sending Asher a scolding glare when he had the audacity to chuckle at her discomfort. "Have you no shame?"

"You two ought to get a room," the parking attendant called out to them.

"And you ought to mind your own business," Asher fired back, at which the attendant ducked his head and ambled back to his glass cube.

"Dana said you were bad news and she's right. I want you to stay away from me, Asher Ames."

"Don't listen to Dana. I haven't seen her in years. How can she know anything about me?"

"She was rather close to you in college, or have you conveniently forgotten that you two were pinned for a couple of months?"

"I haven't forgotten, but that's old news, Tess. I won't hold you responsible for your actions back in college if you don't hold me responsible for mine." He propped the heel of one hand against her car and dazzled her with one of his smiles. "I don't know why, but I like you. I always have. I like your moxie and the way your nose turns up on the end." He smiled when she crossed her eyes to get a look at the tip of her nose. "And I like your sense of humor . . . most of the time, anyway. What do you like about me?" He kissed her quickly, stunningly, before she could speak. "And 'my absence' isn't a valid answer. You can do better than that."

She sighed and leaned her forehead against his, feeling as if she'd just run a race. "You're reading my mind. That's dangerous."

"Answer me. What do you like about me?"

"Ash, please . . ."

"I don't buy that bit about us being professional enemies, you know. I think you're running away from me because you feel that old black magic. I feel it, too, Tess. In my bones . . . and in other strategic places, as well."

"I'm not going to do this, Asher." Tess drew a breath, feeling her head begin to swim. She straightened and her swift movements forced him to back off. "I'm not going to start something with you that I know will get me nowhere."

"How can you know that?"

"I just know." *You don't know anything*, a voice teased inside her head. *All you know is that Asher Ames has your number, and he keeps punching it in and you keep picking up the receiver!* She wrenched open the car door and tossed her briefcase and the computer case inside. "We already have a working relationship that's about as stable as a load of nitroglycerin, making any other kind of relationship simply out of the question." She flung him a puzzled glance. "I don't know why you can't see that, and I can't figure out why you're being so . . . so . . . tenacious!"

"Because I want you. Simple enough?"

She regarded him for a few breathless moments, numbed by his frank statement. How handsome he was in the waning light of day, with the sun's afterglow caught in his silvery eyes and the shadows of evening pooled beneath his cheekbones! She had dreamed of him in college—dreamed of him against her will. Later she had wondered why his memory haunted her. She'd told herself that he represented lost causes, but now she wondered if her obsession might have been firmly rooted in pure, mindless lust. Because she was feeling it now. Feeling it in her heart, her head, her every throbbing pulse. It would be so easy, so simple to give herself up to the drumming beat of her desire—

"It's not that simple," she said, more to herself than to him, then she slid onto the car seat. She grabbed the door handle, but Asher kept her from closing herself in. "Please, let go."

"Are you going to Las Vegas?"

"Am I . . . ?" She snapped her jaws shut, realizing she was on the verge of stuttering. "Probably not."

He tipped his head to one side, and she felt he was staring through her, seeing her most secret self.

"Chicken," he said with a sly smile. "How can you compete with me if you're not even in the same league? Any entertainment writer worth his or her salt will be there."

"It's just a bunch of hype staged by the networks," she said, amazed she could sound so convincing when she didn't believe a word of what she was saying. "You're placing too much importance on it."

"If it's not important, then why have you gone every year since you've been on the newspaper?" he asked, collapsing her house of cards. "You wouldn't stay behind just because I'm going, would you?"

"Don't flatter yourself," Tess said, starting her car and looking for a quick getaway. She flung back her hair in what she hoped was a carefree gesture, then she released a volley of laughter that didn't quite ring true. "You really should watch that ego of yours, Asher. If it gets much bigger, you'll have to claim it as a dependent come tax time."

She steered the car from the lot, leaving Asher behind, but unable to escape thoughts of him so easily. The heavy traffic gave her plenty of stops and starts and time to think about her whirlwind reunion with him. By the time she finally reached her apartment, a headache had settled behind her right eye. She took two aspirin before sitting at the kitchen table to eat her cheeseburger and fries. The food was tasteless and she threw most of it down the garbage disposal. Depression colored her mood, making her whole world seem gray.

"What's wrong with me?" she asked, moving listlessly to her bedroom and doing a belly flop onto the bed. She bounced, then settled more comfortably as she tried to recall her last date—not counting that evening out with Asher. It had been months ago, she realized. She'd gone out with a local television news anchor. "Ugh," she grunted, remembering how he'd preened the night away and kept the conversation centered on him. "Never again," she vowed.

That's why she didn't go out and kick up her heels more often! Men like that news anchor were the cause of her frustration. Give me a good book and a diet cola any night, she thought with conviction. She wasn't averse to having a night out with an attractive, intelligent male, but where were they hiding? If they were in those singles bars, then forget it. She'd rather visit a rattlesnake nest than spend an hour in one of those meat lockers.

And as for the office, it was slim pickings. Most of the bachelors were single for good reason. One of the available guys there had been divorced for the third time last year. *Three women can't be wrong*, Tess thought with a stab of amusement.

What was left? Join a singles group, a bowling league? Hang out in menswear at her favorite department store? It wasn't easy being single, she concluded. It was hard to meet a nice guy in a big city. . . . But wait a minute! She sat up, stung by the realization that she'd never felt being single was a burden until lately. A few weeks ago she'd been happy playing solitaire. She'd even thought herself lucky to come home to peace and quiet, not having to fight someone for the television remote control or prepare a meal for someone who took her for granted.

So why was she making excuses for herself now? Why did she feel as if something were missing in her life? Just because Asher had said she needed more fun in her life—an affair, to be exact—didn't mean she should automatically doubt her chosen life-style.

Falling onto her back, Tess stared up at the ceiling. Did she choose her life-style or did it choose her? she wondered.

An affair. The man had actually suggested that she have an affair! Of course, he hadn't said she should have one with him, but the implication had most certainly been there.

He's the competition, she reminded herself. *Forget his kisses and the way his eyes get all silvery when he looks at you. Forget all that, and remember that the newspaper business is a dog-eat-dog world.*

"A love affair," she murmured as her heartbeat accelerated. "A love affair with none other than Asher Ames himself."

Dana would probably try to have her committed.

4

POUNDING AWAY at the lap-top computer's keyboard, Tess furrowed her brow and buried herself more deeply in the play review she was crafting on the green screen. She paused, plucked a juicy adjective from her own mental storage system and planted it in the next sentence. Perfect, she judged with a nod.

She leaned back against the couch and reached for the carryout cup of iced tea. Slightly off target, she sent the cup sideways. The plastic lid didn't hold, releasing the remains of the tea across her coffee table and over her notes and newspapers.

"That was swift, Maxwell," she groused, and tried to wipe up the mess with the paper bag her fries and cheeseburger had come in. Nonabsorbent, the sack just smeared the liquid, and Tess headed toward the linen closet for a towel. On the way, she realized she'd splashed tea on the front of her white shirt, as well. "Way to go, Grace," she whispered, grabbing a towel from the stack. She hurried back to the living room, but a knock on her door detoured her.

"Now what," she grumbled, pressing her eye to the peephole. When she saw a fish-eye view of Asher, she stumbled backward and forgot about the spilled tea and the film review and how to breathe. The knocking came again and galvanized her. "What do you want?" she called, then winced when she heard the drill sergeant's tone of her voice. "I mean . . . I'm not decent."

"I know, that's why I like you."

Tess looked through the peephole again. Just as she'd thought. He was grinning from ear to ear.

"Tess, please open the door. I won't bite if you won't."

The decision to open up came when she realized his voice carried not only into her apartment, but into every other one along the corridor. She released the lock and let him in.

"You could have phoned first," she said, dabbing at the wet spots on her shirt with the towel, and then she remembered the accident. "S'cuse me," she murmured, shunting past him to wipe up the tea. While she was at it, she stored her story on the disk and switched off the computer.

"Ah, so you were writing," Asher observed, delivering a lopsided grin as his gaze moved over the wasteland that was her coffee table. He sniffed the air. "There's nothing quite as clinging as hamburger grease. Cheeseburger and fries, right? Do you dine in every night?"

"No, of course not." She stacked some papers, kicked a few magazines under the coffee table and then shrugged in defeat. "I wasn't expecting company and it's the maid's night off."

"Right. Sure." His smile removed the sting from his droll tone. "And I just happened to be in the neighborhood and decided to stop in for a chat even though I had scads of other social engagements penciled in for to-night."

Tess opened the sliding glass door and draped the wet towel over the railing to dry. The night was cool but pleasant, and she was glad when Asher followed her out onto the small balcony. He sat in one of the metal chairs and directed his gaze upward to where tree branches mingled and whispered to the stars.

"Nice night."

"Yes, it is," Tess agreed, taking the other chair. She stretched out her legs and crossed them at the ankles, wishing he'd given her a little advance notice so she could have changed out of her sweatpants. "Want something to drink?"

"No, thanks." He closed his eyes and sighed. "I like it here. I think I'll spend the night."

She whipped her gaze around to him, saw the sparkling mischief in his eyes, and released a spate of laughter that cracked the wall of tension his visit had constructed.

Tess flapped a hand at him. "You're so full of bull it's a wonder you aren't tagged and branded."

He wrinkled his nose, "Oh, you're no fun," he complained. "Actually, I came by to run an idea past you." He shifted to one hip, twisting around in the chair to face her. "Since we're both going to Las Vegas—"

"I never said I was going," she reminded him.

"I thought we'd cut costs by sharing a room while we're there. What do you think? Sounds like a blast, doesn't it?"

"I give up." She bounded up from the chair, feeling her cheeks sting as visions of her and Asher in a queen-size bed danced in her head. Before she could escape, he caught her hand, gave a quick yank and had her in his lap before she could so much as utter a protest. "Oh, no, you don't," she said, eluding his searching mouth.

"One kiss. One, itty-bitty kiss. What can it hurt?" he wheedled.

Laughing under her breath, she shook her head. "You're shameless. Well . . ." She regarded his handsome face, so close to hers that she could feel the warmth of his breath. "I hate to see a man beg." She gave in and rested her mouth comfortably on his.

The lightheartedness of the moment evaporated, and what had started as a friendly jest quickly became a serious quest for fulfillment. The shock of his tongue invading her mouth alarmed her at first, then triggered a desire that swept through her like a fire storm. Tess arched into him, her body instinctively seeking a connection. She raked her hands through his hair, setting off an avalanche of yesterday's fantasies—fantasies of kissing him, holding him, driving him wild with wanting. Denying those fantasies seemed utterly ridiculous now that her mouth surged against his and her arms wound around his neck with fierce possessiveness. His tongue stroked hers and tickled the roof of her mouth. She moaned as heat built between her thighs, making her aware of just how desperately she wanted Asher Ames.

But she wasn't the only one betrayed by her body. After all, she was sitting in his lap. She felt him grow and throb.

Tess tore her lips from his and forced herself to stand. She held to the railing, needing its support. Her face felt hot, her lips swollen, her breasts full. He stood behind her and placed his hands on the tops of her shoulders, squeezing gently.

"Why is it that we can't exchange itty-bitty kisses?" he asked, amusement threading through his voice.

"I guess we do everything in excess."

"I don't have this problem with other women."

"And there have been scores of them, right?"

"Hundreds. Thousands, even."

"Ha." She looked back at him, sharing a smile. "And I'm the first one to arouse you, is that what you're telling me?"

"Well, not exactly, but you're the first woman in a long, long time who can make me crazy with just one kiss."

"I'm flattered, I guess."

"You should be." His hands slipped from her shoulders and down her arms. "I'm looking forward to Las Vegas, aren't you?"

"I'm not sure. Ash, I'm just not ready for this . . . for you, I mean. I feel like I'm punch-drunk."

"I'm flattered, I guess."

She turned around in his arms. "There's a lot of water under the bridge, and mixing business and pleasure is like mixing oil and water."

"And a stitch in time saves nine, and an apple a day keeps the doctor away," he teased.

Tess sighed, realizing she did sound like a book of clichés. "What I'm trying to say is that, for now, I think we should be friends. That's it. That's enough."

"That's enough?" He stuffed his hands into his pockets and sent her a disbelieving look. "I don't think so. I think you want me as much as I want you. In fact, I think we wanted each other back in college, but we were either too shy or too stubborn to admit it."

"You were Dana's guy, remember?"

"Yes, but that didn't stop me from liking you."

"You liked me?"

"Yes. What about you?" He dipped his head to arrest her gaze. "Didn't you think I was kind of cute?"

She tried not to smile, but couldn't stop herself. "Kind of. I don't remember."

"Oh, sure," he said, his tone challenging. "And I suppose you don't remember sharing a blanket with me at the homecoming game when you were a sophomore."

"I . . . I . . ." Tess forced herself to shut up and stop stuttering. "I remember," she confessed, her mind vividly painting that day and those hours. Too few of them. She could once again feel the wicked nip in the air and the warmth of Asher's body against hers under the plaid stadium blanket. "Dana was an attendant," she said. "That's how we ended up sitting together during halftime."

"Yes, we sat together to watch the queen and her procession on the field. It was cold and you were shivering, so I told you to snuggle under the blanket with me and you did." He pulled one hand from his pocket and laid it against the side of her face. "And I thought I was going to die of pure lust."

"You...really?" She couldn't believe it. She'd thought she'd been the only one writhing with unrequited desire that day. Tess lowered her gaze, and her lashes caressed the tip of his little finger. "You never let on."

"How could I? I was supposed to be Dana's boyfriend." He kissed her, his lips lingering lightly, sweetly. "I wanted to kiss you that day and every day after that."

"I find that hard to believe." She edged away from him, moving from the balcony into her apartment. A clinging, cloying sensation coated her heart and she felt vulnerable. Was he playing with her, making fun of her tender feelings? She couldn't be certain... not of anything. "You haven't been pining for me, Asher Ames, and you know it. I can't guess what you're up to, but I think you should go. I've got work to do." She stood beside the coffee table and stared blindly at the portable computer. For the life of her, she couldn't remember what she'd been writing about before he'd dropped in.

"Maybe I wasn't completely knocked off my feet by you back in college, and maybe I haven't been pining away for you since then, but I'll tell you one thing you can bank on, my Moxie Maxie." He cradled her chin in one hand and brought her face around to his. "Friendship is a beginning, but it's not enough for me. Not where you're concerned. We're good for each other."

"How do you figure that?" Tess asked, telling herself she could lift her chin from his hand, but unable to find the willpower to do it.

"We keep each other teetering on the edge."

"And that's good?"

"The best." He kissed the tip of her nose. "It's called chemistry, sweetheart." His mouth touched hers as he tacked on, "Sexual chemistry. Sex," he whispered, his lips imprinting the word on hers. "You know about sex, don't you?"

"It comes after five, doesn't it?"

His laugh felt good on her lips, too. Too good. Tess took a step back, breaking the spell he'd cast. Sensing her newfound resolve, he shrugged in defeat and went toward the door. He dropped an envelope onto the end table as he passed it.

"I'll just leave those with you."

"What . . . what's this?" Tess asked, reaching for the envelope.

"Tickets to the local production of *Carmen*."

"No. Uh-uh. No way. I'm not going with you, so you can just forget it. Take these with you." She extended the tickets, but he ignored her, already halfway out the door.

"I'll pick you up."

"Wait . . . Asher."

"Got to run. Bye." The door ended the discussion.

Tess pulled the two balcony tickets from the envelope and tapped them against her fingertips. She could return the tickets, she thought, but she knew she wouldn't. And so did he, damn him.

"YOU LOOK INCREDIBLE," Asher said, standing back from Tess so he could get a better look at the evening gown that hugged her body, showcasing a figure Asher was finding more and more delectable. He saw her shape in everything of late; in hourglasses, patterns in neckties, configurations of clouds.

Tess waited patiently on the threshold of her apartment for him to get an eyeful. Her chocolate brown evening dress had a knee-length full skirt and a strapless, draped bodice. She'd swept her tawny hair up into a casual style that had taken half an hour to create. Pearls circled her neck and clustered at her earlobes.

"And look at you," she said, her gaze moving over his dark blue suit, tailored for evening. His hair was carefully styled, still showing the furrows left by a comb. "I read your review of *Carmen* yesterday. I'm glad you liked it, too."

He angled an elbow at her, and she tucked her hand into the crook of his arm. "It'll be nice seeing it again just for the fun of it. No notes, no checking the spelling of names against the program, no attention paid to audience reaction. Just you and me and the performance."

"I agree. This is a good idea."

"It's about time we agreed on something," he said, holding the outside door open for her. "I couldn't believe that you actually liked the new Freshour film."

"I couldn't believe you didn't," Tess said. "I think Sid Freshour has a knack for directing comedy."

"Comedy of errors, yes." He opened the car door for her and held her hand as she settled into the bucket seat. "You must have been blindfolded when you sat through the d'Antoniono film."

She waited for him to slide into the seat beside her before she answered his challenge. "I wish I had been. You're one of those critics who thinks subtitles mean it's a great film."

"That's not true."

"Name one recent foreign film you haven't praised to high heaven."

"Uh . . . give me a sec."

"I'll give you a whole minute. You won't be able to come up with one."

"Oh, hell. I can't think and it's your fault."

"*My* fault?"

"Yes. What's that perfume you're wearing? It's driving me nuts, making me hot."

Startled by his raw admission, Tess turned her gaze fully on him. He ran a finger under his stiff white collar to pull it and the dark bow tie away from his skin. His gaze darted to hers, then away. The corners of his mouth tipped down, weighted by irritation.

"It's called 'Erotic,'" she said, dimpling at the irony.

"It is." He jiggled his head, clearing it. Glancing her way again, he wished he hadn't when his hungry eyes focused on the slight rise of her breasts above the dress's heart-shaped bodice. His mouth went dry, and he forced himself to think about something else besides wondering if her nipples were pink or brown. "Did you read my interview with Schultz this morning?" he asked, referring to one of the network vice presidents.

"Yes, I read it."

"He's certain the directors won't strike."

"Yes, he told me the same thing last week."

"He did? Why didn't you print it?"

She shrugged. "He doesn't know what he's talking about, that's why. He told me the writers wouldn't strike the day before they did. Schultz sits in his ivory tower and doesn't know what the troops are doing in the trenches. He's spouting wishful thinking, Asher."

Asher frowned. "We'll see. I bet he's right."

"If he is, it'll be a first."

"Anyway, your job isn't to second-guess, Tess. Your job is to report what's said."

"Since when is your job to tell me how to do mine?" she snapped, twisting around to glare at him.

"Let's not do this." He lifted one hand, holding back her anger. "We're going to have a quiet evening. Let's agree to stay off the subject of our work or anything remotely related to it."

"Agreed." She faced front again and saw that they'd arrived at the concert hall, where the traffic was heavy and slow moving. Asher steered the car into the line inching toward a parking garage. She chanced a glance at him. He'd propped his elbow against the door so that he could cradle his chin in his palm. His fingers drummed against his temple, and his eyes were darkly reflective. "What's wrong?" Tess asked. "Can't you think of anything to say now that our work is off-limits?"

"It's not easy," he admitted with a brief chuckle. "I suppose one might say we're married to our work."

"I'm not married to it, but I've been going steady with it for a while," Tess said. "And lately I've been thinking of looking for a new spouse."

"Oh? Thinking of settling down? Who did you have in mind? Is there still time for me to put in an application?"

"Down, boy. I'm thinking about changing jobs," she corrected with a patient smile. "Besides, I've heard that you're not the spouse type."

"Dana again, I suppose." He delivered a quick frown of disapproval. "You should be more careful who you talk to. Back to this stuff about changing jobs...did this happen before or after I moved to Kansas City?"

"Both." She fidgeted with her evening purse, giving herself time to select her words carefully. She didn't want to tip her hand and reveal that she'd wanted his job and had almost had it in her grasp before he'd snatched it away. "You've no doubt noticed the pittance of space I'm given daily?" She glanced around to catch his nod. "More and more I feel hemmed in. There's so much I want to write, but no space. I can't tell you how many articles I've shelved because I didn't have room for them on my entertainment page. It's frustrating."

"Sure it is, especially for someone with your talent."

Tess studied him carefully, searching for any sign of sarcasm, but there was only sincerity in his expression. "You think I'm talented?"

He looked around at her, saw the expectancy in her eyes and chuckled to himself. "Hell, no. I don't think you have a scrap of talent." Throwing her a disgruntled glare, he added, "Of course, I think you're talented, you nitwit. Always have. Always will. Like wine, you get better with age."

"I wasn't fishing . . . I just wanted to know."

"So, now you know." He released a sigh of thanks when he finally maneuvered the car into the garage and past the parking attendant, who waved him to the back rows where a few spaces were still available on the lower level. "Looks like everybody's here. It wasn't this full on opening night."

"Of course not. Everyone was waiting to read our reviews before they bought their tickets."

He tapped his temple and gave a wink. "Good thinking. Say, after *Carmen* I thought we'd go to Inner Circle at the Press Club for drinks."

Tess lifted her brows, impressed with his choice. "Sure. Sounds like fun. I haven't been there since last year's press awards banquet. The bar and grill is my usual hangout."

"Mine, too, but tonight we'll splurge." His gaze arrested hers. "You won't mind being seen with the competition?"

"At the press club?" She laid a hand on his sleeve and wrinkled her nose becomingly. "Ash, honey, you show me a roomful of news hounds and I'll show you a roomful of rivals."

He considered this a few moments before nodding his agreement. "We'll fit right in."

THE INNER CIRCLE was a level above the noisy bar and grill where most of the press corps gathered. Quiet elegance reigned upstairs, attended to by silent waiters and efficient bartenders, who never even clinked a glass.

Commonly known as the Press Club, the establishment was actually listed as Midtown Grill and Supper Club, but since the press had adopted it, the name had fallen into disuse and the nickname had won out. Even the directory listing used both the formal and informal names.

The upstairs supper club was doughnut-shaped, with the oak-and-stained-glass bar in the middle and the kitchens tucked away in the floor above. Instead of having the help run upstairs for the meals, dumb waiters were used to lower the selections for the waiters to whisk to the diners.

Tess and Asher were seated at a reserved table by plate-glass windows that afforded them views of Crown Center and several bubbling fountains.

"Did you ever see that movie *Three Coins in the Fountain*?" Tess asked after they'd ordered.

"Yes." His smile was rueful.

"I love that movie."

"Well, it was entertaining in its day I suppose."

"Oh, I know it's not the kind of thing a man can understand, but let me tell you, it gets to women."

"Like romance novels," Asher suggested.

"Exactly," Tess agreed, then couldn't help but add a few more things most men couldn't begin to fathom. "And being ruled by monthly cycles and giving birth."

He made a face. "Yes, well, we men have our war novels, shoot-em-up flicks and girlie magazines. Guess we have to allow some difference and inequalities between the sexes."

"Makes life interesting."

"That it does." His gaze lingered, heated her skin, made her look away nervously. "In this light your eyes are the color of jade. *Real* jade. The pea-green color, not that darker shade."

"I'll file that away," she murmured, uncomfortable with his intense scrutiny. "Let's see...." Tess forced herself to meet his lambent gaze. "Your eyes are charcoal. Darker than usual."

"Wonder why?" His smile said it all, relaying without question the effect she had on him.

"Uh...because you're hungry?" she ventured, trying to get his mind off her.

"That's right." Now his smile was feral. "Starving. Ravenous. Voracious. Fam—"

"I get the picture," she said, cutting him off and pretending great interest in the few couples on the dance floor. A piano player provided mood music. "Dana said—"

"Dana," he said, making the name an insult. "Why must she always come between us?"

"She isn't. Boy, when you break off with someone, you really break off, don't you? Can't even stand to hear her name."

"What's she doing now?" he asked, forcing himself to be polite.

"She's busy being a single parent. She's divorced, you know."

"No, I didn't."

"Yes, two years now. She has a daughter and a son, my godchildren. Dana works part-time at the hospital in the gift shop. Her ex-husband has been generous, so she's not having too hard a time financially."

"Bully for her."

"What's wrong? Are you still sore she's not your girl?"

"Please." He sighed, shaking his head with derision. "Dana and I were never that tight. We only went together six or seven months, total. She was never much of a challenge." His eyes sparked with interest. "And I love a challenge, Tess."

"She told me everything, you know."

"Everything?"

Tess nodded. "After every date I received a play-by-play commentary."

"Then you know I'm dynamite in bed, right?"

Warm color pooled in her cheeks, and she would have sworn the temperature in the room jumped ten degrees. "Wonder when we'll be fed?" She stiffened when his hand closed on hers.

"They're playing our song."

"Our song? I don't even know the name of it."

"It's got something to do with moonlight and music...."

"Doesn't ring a bell...."

"And French kisses and black lacy underwear."

She frowned but felt laughter bubble in her throat. "You wear that kind of underwear, do you?"

"Want to find out?"

"Not here."

"Then let's dance."

"No," Tess said, tossing a weak smile at him, then sending him a questioning look when he stood up and held out his hand. "No, thanks," she repeated.

"But I'll look silly dancing alone." He captured her hand and pulled her up from the chair. "Be a sport, Maxie."

Under normal conditions, Tess loved to dance, but conditions were never normal around Asher Ames. She felt abnormally stiff in his arms, abnormally clumsy following his lead and abnormally aware of every move and each brush of his body against hers. When she chanced a look at his face, his slumberous expression made her abnormally weak-kneed. Passion shuttered his eyes and parted his lips. His dance steps became more languid with less step and more snuggle. Somehow his lips found the curve of her neck and followed the line to the top of her shoulder. Tess shivered; Asher smiled. Tess inched back; Asher inched forward. Tess tried to look aside; Asher brought her gaze around to his with a steady hand beneath her chin.

"You're going to Las Vegas, aren't you?"

"I don't know," she hedged.

"Tell me. Tell me now." His mouth brushed hers, and his other hand pressed the small of her back.

"I haven't made up my mind," she insisted.

His mouth lingered longer this time. "You're going."

She started to beat around the bush again, but his mouth clung to hers. The tip of his tongue painted her trembling lips. When the kiss ended, the decision was made.

"Yes, I'm going to Las Vegas."

"Good." He glanced sideways. "Our dinner has arrived." But he didn't let her go immediately. "I can hardly wait to be alone with you in Las Vegas."

"We won't be alone, Asher. It's a business convention, remember?"

"Yes, but this time it will be different. This time I think I'll be more interested in satyriasis than in the networks' series and specials."

"What?" Tess shook her head. "You lost me. I'm not familiar with that word."

He touched his lips to the shell of her ear. "When you get home, look it up. I think you'll find its meaning very illuminating, if not downright distracting."

"SATYRIASIS . . ." Tess murmured, dictionary in the lap of her evening dress. Asher had been gone only a minute, having left her at her apartment door with a chaste kiss that left her wanting more. Much, much more.

"How do you spell it?" she asked herself, having trouble locating the word. "Ah, here it is." She aimed a forefinger at it and ran her nail along the definition as she carefully absorbed the meaning. The import of it rocketed through her and caused her heart to beat in double time.

Tess slammed the dictionary shut and squirmed with an odd mixture of embarrassment and titillation. After a few minutes, she let the big book slide from her lap, and she lounged back on the couch. A smile curved her lips and she released a long, luxurious sigh.

"Oh, Las Vegas," she whispered as she closed her eyes to let her fantasies overtake her. "I sure hope you're ready for us."

5

STANDING BEFORE the floor-to-ceiling windows in her hotel room, Tess looked down upon the glitter of the Las Vegas strip. Even in broad daylight it dazzled, it danced, it retained its unabashed gaudiness.

Unpacked and registered, Tess savored the time alone, knowing full well that soon the convention and its participants would sweep her into a whirl of activity. She berated herself for taking pains not to be booked on the same flight out of Kansas City as Asher. It wasn't like her to run from a challenge. Usually she dug herself in and faced whatever bedeviled her, but not this time. It was tough facing temptation itself, and that's what Asher was to her.

She wondered where he was. He'd arrived hours before her; she'd taken the late flight, he the early morning one. She'd had every intention of asking for his room number at the desk, but Lenny Bernard, a critic from Houston, had happened by and waylaid her.

Turning from the window, she eyed the phone. No time like the present, she told herself, while another voice chided her for even wanting to know his proximity.

Punching the desk button, she waited through four rings before a pleasant-voiced man answered the summons.

"Desk."

"Could you give me Asher Ames's room number, please?"

"I'm sorry. We don't give out room numbers. I can connect you to his room, if you wish."

"No!" Hearing the panic in her voice, she winced. "No, thank you."

"Then would you like to leave a message?"

"No. No, thanks anyway." Tess replaced the receiver decisively and tried to melt the phone with her glare. "Oh, well. That means he can't find out my room number, either," she said, consoling herself.

She spent a few minutes in front of the dresser mirror, repairing her makeup and brushing her hair, then went downstairs for a drink and to find her circle of friends: Lenny from Houston, Mike from Pittsburgh, Justin from Atlanta and Steve from Boston. Over the past three or four years, they'd met at the network unveilings and traded industry gossip, hoisted a few drinks and scouted out the best restaurants and dinner shows. Tess had taken one step into the bar when she heard her name shouted from some dark corner. Straining her eyes, she caught sight of Lenny's balding head and she lifted a hand to wave.

Sliding past knots of people, she made her way over to the table. Mike stood up, sporting a new mustache. And there was Steve, wearing one of his terribly busy ties. And Justin! So cute, so boyishly handsome, it was a shame he was happily married.

Laughing with the joy of seeing them again, she let herself be wrapped in Lenny's embrace first, then like a new toy, she was passed from one man to the next. From Lenny to Steve, from Steve to Mike, from Mike to Justin and from Justin to . . . these arms weren't only friendly, they were familiar. Struggling out of them, Tess stared, flabbergasted, at Asher.

"You!"

"Asher asked to join us," Lenny explained. "Since you two are old friends, we welcomed him to our table. That's okay, isn't it?"

Tess turned her back on Asher to face her other friends. "I guess so. Justin, make room. I want to sit between you and Steve." Bulldozing her way around the small table, she offered a smile of thanks to Mike and Justin, who were forced to stand and let her slide onto the bench to sit next to Steve. Everyone settled back into their places. Asher sat in a chair directly across from her.

Dressed in dark slacks and a white shirt, his gray-and-black tie pulled casually off to one side, Asher kept his gaze on her as the others chattered, anxious to catch up on what had transpired since their last rendezvous. Tess made a convincing pretense of hanging on every word and responding with bright enthusiasm, but most of her conscious mind was possessed by Asher and his unwavering attentiveness. At times she had to grind her teeth to keep from shouting across the table at him to quit staring at her. Her nerves were stretched to the limit, and consequently she laughed too loudly, tried too hard and drank too much.

By midnight she was past tipsy, approaching topsy and within shouting distance of turvy.

When the toe of a shoe inched up the cuff of her slacks and slicked her ankle and the back of her leg, she didn't have to guess its owner. Her gaze clashed with Asher's. He grinned; she frowned. He wiggled his eyebrows; she lowered hers.

"Am I in your way?" she asked sweetly. Too sweetly.

"No. Not at all," Asher answered smoothly.

"Good." Cocking her other leg, she sent the toe of her shoe into his shin.

"Oww!" Asher yelped.

"What's wrong?" Lenny asked, and the others fell into a concerned silence.

"I'm sorry," Tess said. "I thought an insect was crawling up my leg. I had no idea it was your foot."

The other men chuckled, ducked their heads and elbowed each other while Asher glowered across the table at Tess. The shoe retreated, and Tess wet one forefinger and made a mark in midair.

Examining the half-empty goblet before her, she realized she'd had one too many White Russians. Shoving the drink aside, she blinked hard to correct her double vision. Asher's smirks became one. Her head cleared long enough for her to deduce that if she wanted to make it to her room under her own power, it was now or never.

"I hate to be a party pooper, but I have to say adieu," she said, and to her ears her voice sounded loose around the vowels. "No, no, really," she insisted when her gentlemen friends chorused complaints. "Seriously, I'm dead tired." She placed a hand to her forehead and tried to think. "What time are the opening remarks?"

"Eight-thirty," Justin said, and everyone groaned.

"Let me out of here," Tess said, giving Justin a shove, and like dominoes the men fell out of the booth and stood none too steadily as she made her exit. Even Asher didn't try to detain her.

The elevator soared up and deposited her on the ninth floor. She found her room, inserted the plastic card in the slot by the door and then pushed into the quiet, cool room.

"Ahh!" Tess fell back on the queen-size bed and kicked off her low heels. She closed her eyes and the bongo players in her head eased up on their punishing rhythm. The calypso beat meandered into a samba and was moving toward a lullaby when a new hammering commenced.

Tess grabbed her head in both hands and pulled it and the rest of her up off the bed. She glared in the direction of the jackhammer noise.

"Who is it?" she barked, only then realizing that whoever was trying to get her attention wasn't in the corridor, but in the room next to hers. She went toward the connecting door with trepidation, turning an ear in its direction to make out the voice that drifted through it.

"Open up, says me."

Recognizing Asher's voice, Tess moaned and rested her throbbing forehead against the door. "Asher, how did you manage it? Out of all the rooms in this hotel, you had to get that one. Life is not only unfair, it's torture."

"Open the door, Tess."

"No way. I'm beat."

"I've got aspirin."

Aspirin. A buoy thrown to a drowning woman. Naturally she hadn't packed any and the hotel drugstore was closed. Tess turned the lock to let him in, but didn't wait around to witness his smirk. She was sitting on the bed when the door swung out and Asher stepped in.

If anything, he looked better than he had ten minutes ago. With his shirt unbuttoned and hanging open and loose, his tie totally discarded and his belt unbuckled, he was masculinity personified. A lock of dark hair hung in a thick comma on his forehead. The hair on his chest, black and plentiful, swirled and dipped to his navel and below. In one hand he held a glass of water and in the other, two aspirin. He propped a shoulder against the door frame, lounging there for a minute to appraise her condition, then he came toward her, offering the medicine and a lopsided smile of commiseration.

Tess took the aspirin and washed it down with the water, ever watchful of his every move. It wasn't that she didn't trust him. She didn't trust herself. Even as she built a wall of indifference around her heart, her pulses pounded anew, no longer a samba, but a racy Latin rhythm.

"I paid off the desk clerk to put you in the room next to mine," he said, giving a tardy answer to her question.

"I should have known." She forced her gaze up to his, but the trip included attractions such as a stomach and pecs many a twenty-one-year-old hunk would envy. "You've horned in on my privacy and my friends. Congratulations, the conference hasn't even started, but you've managed to ruin it for me. Happy now?"

He knelt before her and placed his hands on her knees. Although she wore slacks, the contact of his hands and the shock of the warmth his flesh exuded made her flinch and stiffen. If he noticed, he gave no indication of it.

"I don't want to ruin anything for you, Tess. I want us to remember this trip forever, but I want it to be a good memory."

"You want, you want." She rolled her eyes expressively. "What about what *I* want, huh?"

"You want the same."

"Oh, really?" She inserted a cockiness in her tone. "What did I ever do without you telling me how I feel and what I want?" To her everlasting astonishment, he parted her knees and put himself between them. Her reaction was a split second too late, and her thighs pressed his waist instead of each other. "Don't."

"What?"

She pushed at his shoulders. "This. Go back to your room." She squirmed, resisting the loose lasso of his arms around her hips. "I mean it."

"No, you don't."

"I have a headache and I'm not in the mood to joust with you." Futility rose within her and brought the sting of tears. "Why did you have to show up tonight with my friends? I wanted to be with them, not with you." She squirmed, trying to break through the claustrophobia.

"Tess . . . Maxwell!" The commanding tone of his voice cut through her agitation, and she stilled in his arms. "Do you know why you prefer their company to mine?"

"Yes, because I like *them*." Even as she said it, she felt the weight of absurdity on her tongue.

"You like me, too," he told her. "In fact, what we feel goes beyond that, and that's precisely why you wanted to be with them instead of alone with me." He swayed closer, pressing into the vee of her legs, his chest meeting hers, his hands slipping around to the inside of her thighs. "Maybe you're even afraid of being alone with me. Don't you trust yourself, Maxwell?"

She hated it when he read her mind. Tess leaned back, away from his full lips. She could smell him, spicy and warm like something fresh from the oven. Scrumptious.

"Ames, do you mind?" The moxie he admired came to her rescue and imbued her with courage and strength. "I'm sure you noticed that I'm very nearly three sheets to the wind, but if you think you can take advantage of me, forget it. March yourself out the door so I can get some shut-eye. It's almost one in the morning and we've got to be up and about by eight."

For a few panicky moments she thought he might call her bluff and go right ahead and take advantage of her, but he finally lowered his gaze in a gesture of acquiescence. Unfortunately, his gaze dipped and stayed upon her breasts, which were rising and falling rapidly, giving lie to her brave words. He covered one of her breasts with his mouth, wetting her blouse as he tongued her nipple to a stiff peak. She pushed at his shoulders, more from sexual frustration than because she wanted him to stop. His slow smile said it all. With adagio movements, he pushed himself up, his hands slipping sensuously along her thighs and away in just the nick of time, and strolled across the room to the connecting doors.

"I'll be back tomorrow night, you know," he said.

"Maybe I won't be here," she said, recovering from his onslaught.

"Going to sleep somewhere else?"

"Maybe."

He turned on the threshold, his hand resting on the knob, his eyes mocking her. "If you're not here by ten, I'll come looking for you."

"For what? Just what do you think you and I will do after ten o'clock?"

"Conjure up some magic, I hope. Get a start on those sweet memories we were discussing."

"*You* were discussing," she amended. "Magic, huh?" She crossed one knee over the other and leaned back on straight arms. "Did you pack a philter for the occasion?"

"A filter?" he repeated, brow furrowed.

She smiled, suddenly recognizing a comeuppance. "*Philter* with a *p-h*," she volleyed in a sultry whisper. "Look it up."

Baffled, Asher closed the door, forcing himself to move slowly until she could no longer see him, then he darted to his attaché case. He twisted open the locks and threw up the top. Pushing aside schedules and brochures, he found his dog-eared dictionary and thumbed through it to the *Ps. Ph . . . Phi . . . Philt . . .* Ah! *Philter*, he read, then devoured the definition like a scholar deprived of knowledge too long. He read the definition once more, savoring it, before dropping the dictionary back into the briefcase. His grin defined admiration, then yearning and then debauchery. His gaze slipped to the connecting door, and a primitive rhythm not unlike jungle drums invaded his head. The native in him was restless.

ALL THE NEXT DAY his pulses thrummed. In the crowded conference rooms, where one network heavyweight after another vied for media coverage, Asher found his concentration divided between his work and the object of his desire. He noted that her questions were well thought-out and that network presidents and television stars alike recognized her, calling her by name and answering her questions with equal measures of respect and friendliness.

In short, Asher was impressed. He was also in love.

In love? Whoa! Fishing his handkerchief from his jacket pocket, Asher ran it down his damp face, although the air conditioning was more than adequate. He stuffed the handkerchief back into the inside pocket and shoved the *L* word into a far corner of his mind. After all, it was much too grandiose a word to describe his feelings for a woman with whom he hadn't even been to bed, with whom he hadn't even indulged in heavy petting! Infatuated, maybe. Yes, that was better. That word didn't make him break out in a cold sweat.

Trying to be objective, he decided she was one of the most seasoned reporters in a room chock-full of them. She was also one of the few women in the room. Entertainment writers, editors and critics were a fraternal bunch. It was a cushy job, one of the most sought after at any newspaper, magazine, radio or television station. The boys in the boardrooms guarded it jealously. Women rarely broke through their ranks, and when they did one could bet they did it by being so impossibly talented they couldn't be ignored or refused admittance. At the front of that elite pack stood Tess Maxwell.

Dressed in a white linen suit and a shimmering emerald silk blouse against a background of dark suits, she leaped at the eyes. Her hair, gathered into a stunning French braid that showed off the variegated blondness of it, was a halo among lackluster crowns of normal browns, blacks and an occasional brassy blond. When she smiled, she glowed. When she laughed, the room brightened.

Or did it? Asher wondered, looking around him with a sudden self-consciousness. Or was he seeing Tess with a lover's eyes? How could that be when he wasn't her lover? Why was it that he felt closer to her now than he ever had to women he'd been to bed with?

"Who's the blond in white?" the man beside him asked, obviously noticing that Asher was staring at her, too.

"Tess Maxwell."

"Where's she from?"

"Kansas City."

"Well, well. They *do* have some crazy little women there, don't they?" The man smacked his lips. "You know her very well?"

"Well enough." Asher turned cold, forbidding eyes upon him. "Well enough to know she won't be interested."

The man chuckled and adjusted his tie in the way a fellow does right before he makes his move. "You won't hold it against me for trying, will you?"

"I might." Asher tried to beat down the next statement, but it came flying from his heart, unbounded and undaunted. "She's mine, so hands off, bub."

The lascivious man regarded Asher's immobile expression for a few more seconds before ducking his head and easing sideways with a crablike shuffle. Feeling like a lion whose roar had just scattered the younger competition, Asher threw out his chest and gloried in his aggression. Realizing that those around him had begun to shift and move, Asher glanced toward the front of the room to see the speakers filing out by a side door. This event was over, and he hadn't taken one note. Not one. Asher closed his notebook, then slapped a hand against his jacket pocket. His small tape recorder was there, but he'd forgotten to switch it on.

"Swift move, Ames," he muttered to himself, then looked up to encounter a pair of green eyes that made his heart slam into the roof of his mouth. "Maxwell!" His voice cracked like that of an adolescent, and he grimaced.

"Ames!" she mocked, then tossed off an understanding smile. "What do you think of it?"

"Of what?"

She jerked a thumb over her shoulder, indicating the vacant speakers' table. "The announcement."

"Oh . . ." He closed his eyes for a few moments, wishing the floor would open and swallow him. "Great news."

"Great? You're being facetious, right?"

"Right, right. I'm pulling your leg."

She tipped her head to one side to scrutinize him. "You *do* know what I'm talking about, don't you?"

Asher stuck his notebook high up under his arm and then shoved his hands into his pockets. "No, not really. Enlighten me."

"Where were you?" She looked around her, searching for a reason why he couldn't have seen or heard the goings-on.

"Mars. Just tell me, okay?"

"Maybe I should let you read all about it."

"Tess . . ." He grabbed her elbow before she could escape with the information. "Come on. Be a sport. I was busy defending your honor and I missed the big story."

"You were defending *my* honor?" she asked, giving him a dubious scowl. "How so?"

"What was the announcement?"

"If I tell you, will you explain how my honor came into question?"

"It's a deal. Spill it."

"Turner's reviving the movie-of-the-week gimmick."

"Original productions?"

"That's right. He's already signed some major talent. The official news release will be ready by this afternoon's session."

"Movie of the week . . ." He mulled this over a moment and shook his head. "I think that might be better left in the archives."

"Variety is the spice of life, you know. Some of the series ideas are beginning to look like leftovers to a big part of the tube audience." Tess shrugged. "We'll see. So, tell me about defending my honor."

He knew he was blushing. He could feel the heat build in his cheeks and neck, and there wasn't a damn thing he could do about it except act as if he suddenly had a hot flash. Pulling his collar away from his neck, he blew a current of air upward, lifting a lock of hair off his forehead. "It's warm in here. Let's have a drink."

Tess sighed. "Okay, but you're going to tell me if I have to force it out of you at gunpoint."

"I'll tell, I'll tell," he promised, guiding her toward the exit. "I just need to wet my whistle." In the bar, he located a table for two and was relieved to note that none of Tess's pals were present. He ordered a martini and she asked for a Bloody Shame. "Straight tomato juice?" Asher asked. "What's the occasion?"

"Hangover." She rested a hand against her forehead. "And a promise to myself this morning that I wouldn't drink alcohol during the rest of this trip."

"You look fabulous for a woman with a hangover," he observed, letting his gaze stray over her blushing cheeks and dewy mouth. "Kissable."

"My honor. Let's discuss it."

He frowned playfully at her. "You have a one-track mind."

"So do you, but I keep trying to derail you."

Asher laughed, delighted by her quickness. She was an agile fox to his determined hound. The drinks arrived via a comely cocktail waitress, but he barely noticed. He drank greedily, gratefully, while Tess sipped speculatively, expectantly. There was no getting around it, he told himself. He'd opened his big mouth, and the woman was bound and determined to make him bite down on his own foot.

"Okay," he said, making it a weary preamble. "This guy—you wouldn't have found him the least bit attractive, I assure you—this guy was asking about you and making noises about hitting on you, but I scared him off the scent." He shrugged. "That's it. No big deal."

"Let me get this straight. A man was inquiring about me and you told him something that ended his interest."

"No, not exactly. I just told him to ... well, you know."

"No, I don't." She folded her arms and leaned forward intently. "Lay it on the table, Ames. What did you say to him to scare him off the scent, to use your unflattering phrasing."

"I told him ..."

"Yes?"

"I said something like ..."

"Yes?"

"That you were ..."

"Yes, that I was what?"

"Mine."

"Yours?"

"Mine. My woman."

"Your woman." She slumped against the chair as if she'd lost her backbone. "In other words, you fed him a bill of goods and he bought it."

"Yes, I guess that's right." He felt relief. Safe. A-OK. After all, she hadn't bitten his head off or stormed out of the room. He chuckled, lighthearted. "It was kind of funny."

"I'll bet. But how did you defend my honor?"

"Oh, that's just an expression."

"Well, here's another expression." She stood up to glare down at him, making him realize he'd underestimated her reaction. "Don't do me any more favors."

"But you're here to work, not flirt. You said so yourself."

"I've taken care of flirtatious men for years all by myself, Asher Ames. I don't need *you* to run interference for me."

He rose from his chair to reinstate his height advantage. "How about dinner tonight? Just the two of us?"

"No, thanks. I have other plans."

"Going to dine palsy-walsy, are you?"

"Yes. What of it?"

"A nice safe dinner. No flirting. No fondling."

"I didn't say that."

"You didn't have to. You like being with them because they like you in a strictly platonic way."

"Says you."

"Have your friendly little dinner," he jeered, enjoying her growing uneasiness. "But be in your hotel room by ten."

She made a derisive sound and gathered up her purse and briefcase.

"Ten o'clock, Tess," Asher repeated, verbally wiggling under her skin. "On the dot. Don't be late."

Rolling her eyes, she flopped a hand at him. "Sure thing, Ash. You'd better start without me because I'm not wearing a watch."

"Tess." He caught her wrist and her gaze. Affording her a few moments to see that all jesting had been put aside and he was now jarringly serious, he then rubbed his thumb across the inside of her wrist and felt her pulse quicken. "Don't disappoint me, and I promise not to disappoint you."

"Why are you doing this, Asher? Why me?"

He smiled and let go of her, confident now that she'd come back with the unerring accuracy of a boomerang. "I'll tell you tonight."

She swallowed, her throat flexing alluringly. "Tonight," she promised in a sexy, husky whisper, and his pulses answered, renewing their hot thrumming.

6

TESS PACED in her hotel room and thought about life and how queer it could be.

Her memory took her back to college, when she and Dana had been roomies and Asher Ames had been Dana's reality and Tess's dream. She could recall watching him from afar, aching to experience first-hand the kisses Dana had once described as "heavenly and hellish." That description had hounded Tess. Thereafter, every man who kissed her was judged by that intriguing juxtaposition of words, but she found none who could deliver the goods. She was left feeling disenchanted, like a reluctant virgin. What was worse, every time she had looked at Asher, her gaze had been drawn to his mouth—that gently bowed upper lip and the full lower one. It mocked her, taunted her, like a carrot dangling before a hungry beast.

Of course, Asher had been deaf, dumb and blind to her misery, and that had infuriated her even further. Being rejected was one thing, but being ignored was far worse.

Tess checked her watch, then slipped it off and put it on the end table. Quarter of ten. She'd been in her room since eight-thirty, having excused herself promptly after dinner because her stomach was about as steady as a shipboard romance. Wondering if Asher knew she'd been in her room all that time she glanced toward the connecting door. Was he in his room, or had he gone out with friends she hadn't met? He might have made some friends here, but she couldn't imagine when he'd had time. What with all the business meetings and his dogged pursuit of her, when could he have squeezed in socializing?

She shook her head, baffled by it all. Never had she been tracked by a man. She'd been nudged, winked at, tested, but never chased! It was exhilarating, but also puzzling. A man such as Asher—successful, confident and gorgeous—could have any number of women. Did he pursue all with such devotion, or was she special?

He was in hot pursuit and pleading with her to lower the barricades so he could slide right in—into her bed, into her heart. Balling her hands into fists, she wished he'd gone about it differently. This appointed time stuff was hell! Never had minutes ticked by so slowly. What was so special about ten o'clock, for crying out loud? Did he turn into Casanova when the clock struck ten bells?

Infuriating man, making her play by his inane rules. Why should she? Why not make him play by *her* rules, which would make a hell of a lot more sense?

She wouldn't set an exact time for their rendezvous. Whoever heard of such a thing? Was he the kind of man who also appointed certain days for lovemaking?

If he was *that* kind, then he'd have to find another player. She wouldn't be able to tolerate it.

Better to let things happen naturally instead of trying to force her to surrender to his charm. None of this showing up every time she turned around or horning in on her friends. No, none of that. Too calculating for her tastes. Yet another indication of his fondness for timetables. Courting should be freewheeling, no-holds-barred, total serendipity. For as many conquests as he no doubt could claim, the man knew absolutely nothing about romance.

Kicking off her shoes, she tiptoed across the carpet to the connecting door and pressed an ear to it. She heard the distinct opening and closing of the other door, the one opening onto the corridor. Tess straightened, pricked by the realization that Asher had just returned to his room—from where? Had he been with someone else while she'd been pacing like a caged tigress?

Opting for a surprise attack, she left her room and stood outside his. She knocked smartly, then stepped off to one side so he couldn't see her through the peephole. The door swung open and she revealed herself. He was in a business suit, reporter's notebook in hand, and he looked as guilty as sin. Tess's quick glance past him took in the tape recorder on top of his dresser and two minicassettes lying next to it.

"Tess, why didn't you use the connecting door?" he asked, whisking the notebook behind him and out of her view.

"Where have you been?" she asked, crossing her arms loosely in front of her and pitching her weight onto one leg. When he didn't answer immediately, she charged in to fill the silence. "You've been interviewing someone, haven't you?" She uncrossed her arms to send a forefinger into the center of his chest in quick, punctuating jabs. "You've been working," she accused as hotly as a wife would accuse a husband of having a mistress.

For a few seconds it looked as if he might manufacture a lie, but then he seemed to think better of it. Instead, he produced a short laugh meant to belittle her. "Yes, that's right. I'm a reporter and this is a business conference and, yes, I've been working. So what?"

She narrowed her eyes suspiciously. "Who were you interviewing?"

"It doesn't matter. Give me a minute to freshen up and I'll be right—"

"*Who* were you interviewing?"

His mouth twisted into a frown. "Maxwell, I'm not going to tell you. You wouldn't tell me such a thing, either, so don't look so wounded."

"You set me up."

"I what?"

"You set me up," she repeated more heatedly. "You fed me a line about some big seduction scene beginning at ten o'clock, *knowing* I'd be preoccupied by it, and then you slipped out and scooped me! Of all the devious, deceitful—"

"Now hold on a minute," he said, retreating as she advanced into his room to investigate the tapes. When she started to put one into the cassette player, he snatched it from her hand and put it and the other one into the top drawer, which he then closed with deliberate finality. "No, Tess, and you're wrong about this plan I supposedly cooked up. I wasn't planning on this interview. It sort of fell into my lap."

"Fell into your lap? Must have been a woman," she mused, gliding around the room to look for further clues. "A starlet? A full-fledged actress? Someone with a miniseries or a regular series? Someone who wasn't supposed to be here, but showed up after all? No . . . wait! Someone who was leaving without telling anybody and you got an interview before she could disappear. I'm right, aren't I?"

"Let's drop it." He put the notebook into another drawer and closed that, as well. "It's ten o'clock and you know what that means."

"Yes," she said, almost purring, then slipped past him toward the door. "It means it's time for bed." On the threshold, she looked over her shoulder. "Good night, Ash. See you in the morning."

"Maxie . . . come on. . . ."

She closed the door on his weak attempt to lighten her mood and went back to her own room. Slamming the door and hoping the sound rattled his eardrums, she locked it, chained it and resisted piling furniture against it, then she took up her stance at the window, wishing she could sprout wings and fly away.

Of all the rotten things to do, she fumed. The man was impossible. Just when she'd thought he was really interested in her—sincerely attracted to her—he'd tricked her into fantasizing about him while he went behind her back and secured an interview with somebody he obviously thought of as a heavy hitter. Why else would he go to such extremes to keep her occupied while he chased down his real prey? The rat. She'd get him back, she vowed. She'd get an interview or a piece of news that would make him green with envy. Just you wait, she chanted inside. Just you wait, Asher Ames! You won't know what hit you. I'll flatten you. I'll pulverize you. I'll reduce you to—

"I wish I were a camera and could record how you look at this very moment."

Asher's voice shattered her thoughts of revenge, and she jerked her head around to look at him, silhouetted in the open doorway connecting their rooms. *Should have checked the lock on it, stupid,* she told herself. *Dumb, dumb, dumb.* She deserved to be bamboozled by him if she couldn't even keep him out of her room.

He was a dark wide-shouldered bulk with no face, but she felt his steady stare. His words registered a moment before he whispered to her again in a voice that was so sensuously masculine it cut through her defensiveness like a knife through butter.

"The colored lights splashing over your white blouse and across your face...it's beautiful. You're beautiful."

She laughed under her breath, her anger tamed by his flattery. "You wouldn't be so charitable if you knew what I was thinking."

"What?"

She shook her head, loathe to let the words out into the open. "It wasn't kind."

"There was no scheme on my part, Tess. You must believe that. I went downstairs for a drink and . . . well, one thing led to another. In fact, I cut the whole thing short so that I could get back up here by ten."

"Gee, thanks." She tossed off a watered-down smile. Tess squinted against the gloom. "Come into the light. I want to see your face."

"I'll take that as an invitation to stay a while." He stepped into the light thrown by the table lamp.

He'd removed his tie and unbuttoned the first four buttons of his madras shirt. His hair showed a recent finger-combing, and she could picture him running his hands through it in mute frustration caused by her. Good, she thought with a smirk. He *should* feel *something*. It was only fair since she was wound up tight, ready to whirl out of focus.

"You're still my girl, aren't you?" he asked with a boyish smile that was in contrast to the frankly sexual glint in his eyes.

Suddenly whatever courage she had deserted her, and she felt uncertain of her next move. "Well, whatever is done is done," she said, turning away from him for the confusion of color outside. "I'm not really all that mad. It just points out how our jobs keep tripping us up, as I predicted. It's amazing we're friends. I think it's wise if we don't push it, and be satisfied with that."

He moved so quietly, so pantherlike, that she didn't know he was near until his arms came around her, holding her against him as his breath heated the side of her neck.

"I think that's the dumbest thing I ever heard," he whispered, then rested his cheek against hers to stare out at the flashing lights and starry sky above them. "We've come too far to turn back now, don't you think?"

"No." She swallowed thickly, having trouble getting that single word out. Forcing herself to concentrate on what she wanted to say to him and not on how his cheek felt sandpapery against hers, she spoke past her nervousness. "While you were out plying your trade, I was up here—just as you'd expected—wondering why a man like you is so bound and determined to bed a woman like me."

"And what did you come up with?"

"Nothing. You could have chased me in college, but you didn't."

"I didn't know you wanted me to."

"Liar."

"Well, I wasn't sure—of you or of myself back then."

"But you think I want to be chased by you now?"

"You're telling me different?"

The tip of his tongue wet a line up her neck. She closed her eyes in a moment of exquisite torture. "Asher, please, will you just be straight with me for once?"

"I don't like that implication. I *have* been straight with you, Maxie."

She wriggled free enough to spin around and face him. "Just tell me why you're suddenly so darned interested in me. You've lived without me very well. You're handsome, you're successful, you don't want for female company, so what gives? The only thing I can figure out is that you get off on a challenge, but that means this infatuation will vanish once you get me where you want me." Her gaze strayed toward the bed, then bounced back to him.

He propped his hands on his hips and stared at her with open amazement. "Will you listen to yourself? Talk about a lack of self-esteem! Lordy, honey, you take first prize!"

"Just answer the question."

"Okay." He flung out his hands. "Okay, I will." Grabbing her by the wrist, he hauled her across the room to the full-length mirror in the foyer. He made her stand before it as he positioned himself behind her to command her reflected gaze.

"What's this supposed to prove?"

"I'm trying to answer your stupid question," he said testily. "So be quiet." Crouching a little so that his face was level with hers, he looked intently at her mirror image and his eyes became heavy lidded, his mouth loose and inviting. In the blink of an eye he had changed from irritated to seductive. "See that woman in the mirror? I want you to see her through my eyes and then you'll know why I want her... why she has come to mean so much to me." He turned his head just enough to brush a kiss upon her cheek. "You see, I've known her for years, but she's always been untouchable, unattainable. Like a dream."

"You were the unattainable one," she interjected.

"Hush, this is *my* answer, not yours." He cupped her chin in one hand, holding her face still. "Look at her. See those eyes? Limpid green. And the rest of her face is pure fascination. As serene, as mysterious as the Sphinx. And this hair... it's spun gold and I want to feel it all over me. I want to wrap myself in it. Don't laugh," he cautioned when her eyes twinkled. "You don't laugh at a man when he's baring his soul, Maxie. It's just not done."

That sobered her. That socked her in the gut so hard she felt her knees weaken. In the subdued light of the room his eyes were murky and his face mostly in shadow, but she felt the brightness of him, experienced the warmth of him seeping into her bones. She had asked for a serious answer, and by Jove, he was giving her one.

"This woman is intelligent," he went on, rubbing his cheek against hers. That perfume, so aptly named, teased him and sent a message to his groin. He grew hard and pressed against his trousers' zipper. Could she feel him? He snuggled closer so she would. Her eyes widened and he chuckled. "And she's witty and she makes me laugh. That's important. I like to laugh, but I don't do enough of it. But with this woman, I do. I feel happy when I'm around her."

Unable to keep her emotions at bay, tears blurred her vision. She swallowed the lump in her throat, but it came right back.

"She understands me more than she cares to admit, I think. She always has had a direct route to the real me. When I had a falling out with some of my fraternity brothers and I dropped out of the fraternity, she told me that I hadn't wanted to be one of the pack anyway. And you know what? She was right. She knew me better then than I knew myself."

"Ash, we put too much emphasis on things that happened back then, don't you see?" Her head fell back against his shoulder. "We're all grown-up now and—"

"Okay, let's talk about now. Right now I can hardly breathe because I'm so full of wanting. I want you. Only you." His hands wandered, up her arms and then over her breasts. "You can hear it in my voice," he said, his tone dipping to a scratchy whisper that had a throbbing behind it. "You can feel it . . . feel it?" He spread his hands against her stomach and pulled her against him, against the hardness of him. She could only manage a bobbing of her head.

Tess started to close her eyes, but he gave her a little shake and her eyes popped open again.

"Look at us," he ordered. "I want you to see us and then you'll know why this . . . why *we* are meant to be."

Clear-eyed, she watched him unbutton her blouse, part the fabric and cup her lace-covered breasts. Her nipples puckered to kiss his palms. He rubbed his lips against her cheek and then down the side of her neck as he slipped the blouse off her shoulders and let it fall with a sigh to the floor. After removing his shirt, he wrapped her in his embrace, letting her know the leashed power in his muscled arms and chest. She felt small and wonderfully delicate.

His hair-roughened chest tickled her smooth back and shoulders. She ran her hands along his forearms, enjoying the contrast of coarse hair against her damp palms. Tess stood perfectly still, though inside she was a whirlpool of feelings.

The woman in the mirror had large lustrous eyes and a moist, trembling mouth. The man behind her unfastened her bra, worked the straps off her shoulders, then flung it aside. As he took a love bite out of her shoulder, the gentle pressure of his teeth turned up her inner flame. She sucked in breath that whistled into her mouth.

The rise and fall of her pale breasts tempted him; he covered them with his hands and kneaded gently. He took her nipples between his fingers, teasing until she sighed his name.

She reached up behind her and flattened her hands at the back of his head to guide his mouth to the curve of her neck. He found pleasure points she hadn't known existed. Stretching like a cat, Tess surrendered to him.

He unzipped her slacks and pushed them down over her slim hips and thighs, then let them fall by themselves the rest of the way. He caressed her thighs and stroked inside where her skin was hot and tender.

Misty light caught at the silver strands in his raven's-wing hair as he bent his head to feather kisses across her shoulder. She kicked aside her slacks and pirouetted in his arms. He took her mouth with swift supremacy, his tongue surging inside. Nerve endings sizzled and popped as they exchanged openmouthed kisses that grew progressively more frantic. He pulled away first and gasped for breath.

Tess smiled against his moist mouth. He lifted his head so he could see her; he wanted to etch her expression into his memory. Smoothing his palms over her sleek head, he unbraided her hair, and the strands tangled around his fingers and whispered across the back of his hands. When her hair was loose and flowing across her shoulders, he gathered handfuls of it and brought it up to his nose as if it were a bouquet.

"Ah," he breathed. "Better than wine, better than perfume, better than the fairest flower."

"I hope tonight means as much to you as it does to me," she told him, her voice hardly more than a whisper.

"It does," he assured her. Inching his fingers under the elastic circling her hips, he drew down her panties, removing the last vestige of modesty. Then he stepped back to regard her with eyes that glowed feverishly. "In my dreams you weren't this beautiful. I love the freckles across your shoulders and that mole near your left nipple." His gaze lingered on her dark blond delta. "I love everything about you." He let out a ragged breath.

She bowed her body into his and drove her hands up through his silky hair. He kicked off his shoes and then, gently moving her away from him, he unzipped his trousers. His hands fell away to let her do the rest. Reaching inside his open trousers, she found him full of yearning, while he sucked in his breath and grew very still. The slight caress of her fingers sent a shudder through him.

"Tess." Never had her name been uttered with such passion, and it set off a powerful, electric reaction. The moment he spoke it, the atmosphere became charged.

Holding him sent a sensuous current flowing through her, jolting but energizing. With his help, she removed his slacks and underwear, and when released, his sex stretched toward her, seeking her woman's warmth. With desire coursing through her, she gave a little hop and wrapped her legs around his waist, her arms around his neck, her love surrounding him like a warm cloak.

He took her mouth, and they kissed deeply, thoroughly. Passion sizzled through him like a live wire, snaking and writhing, lighting him up inside and then finding outlets in his hands, his lips, his tongue.

"You've been holding out on me, Tess," he murmured, his lips throwing sparks down the column of her throat and between her breasts. "I thought you'd be like brandy, slowly warming, but you're a red hot pepper. Hot, hot, hot," he said, panting the one-word chant.

He carried her to the bed, where the covers were already turned back and waited to be mussed. Tess slipped down his slick body to the bed, and he kissed her again, his tongue making love to her so expertly that Tess felt the buildup of a climax. Each hungry kiss inched up her thermostat until she fell back onto the bed to escape the sweet torture. Asher stretched out on top of her, his body fitting hers like an interlocking piece of a jigsaw puzzle.

His silvery eyes darkened to gunmetal gray as he lowered his hot mouth to her breasts and he bathed them with loving strokes of his tongue. Tess rubbed her heels along his back and buttocks, and her hands traced his shoulder blades and the muscles in his upper arms. She moaned, caught in the maelstrom. All previous notions of loving and being loved dissolved under the heat of his passion. She wanted to cry out with the glory of it all, but she had no voice. She could only relay her pleasure through her own kisses and caresses. When he whispered her name, she knew the sound of angels. When his attention drifted lower and his mouth settled against her, she quaked with longing and arched her back in an unconscious plea for unity.

"Asher, Asher," she whispered, panting his name. "I want you to love me. It's all I've ever wanted."

Mouth upon mouth, belly to belly, fingers threading through fingers, he eased into her. Her gasp was born of surprise, her moan of ultimate pleasure. The way he filled her, so completely, so perfectly, pleased her. She tightened around him, clinging to him as he set a feverish pace that created a friction so divine Tess thought she might faint. But then he stilled as if frozen. She opened her eyes, saw that he was as taut as a bowstring and knew he was on the brink. Then he smiled, groaned, bowed his head, and warmth flooded through her like a shower of sunlight. His release became her own, an echo traded between them, back and forth and back again. He changed her definition of pleasure, of passion, of lovemaking and gave her new yardsticks for them all. Her woman's wisdom told her few, if any, would ever measure up to him.

He was worth the wait.

"Tess, oh, Tess," he whispered against her shoulder. He looked at her and bestowed a sweet suckling kiss to her waiting lips. "Was it worth the wait?"

She blinked, surprised to hear him repeat her own declaration. "Yes, wasn't it?"

"As far as I'm concerned, this is the first time I've made love."

"Oh, Asher," she said, laughing a little.

"Honest." He kissed her again. "It's the first time I've lost myself so completely. For a few seconds I didn't know where I stopped and where you began. Didn't you feel it? That connection. It was...special." He shrugged and uneasiness entered his eyes. "I don't know...maybe I'm full of—"

"Magic," she said quickly before he could finish. "You're full of magic and wonder and wizardly things."

He grinned and pleasure radiated from his expressive eyes. "Honey, you ain't seen nothin' yet," he promised, and then he proved it.

"I KNOW YOU CAN'T BE having second thoughts," Asher said, reaching across the luncheon table for her hand. "Because I *know* the earth moved for both of us and the world looked better than ever this morning and our faces hurt from smiling so much, so I *know* you can't be regretting anything that's happened." Tipping his head to one side, he regarded her intently. "So why do I think I see regret floating in those green eyes of yours?"

Tess squeezed his hand. "The regret isn't about anything that happened. I'm only dreading the time when we have to leave and go back to the real world."

"This is the real world."

"No, not for us. You can't tell me you haven't thought how this, well, *complicates* our working lives."

"Honestly, I haven't given it any thought."

"Honestly?" She shook her head in amazement. "That's *all* I can think about."

"Maybe you think too much." He caressed the top of her hand with his thumb. "Why not shut off your mind and let your feelings guide you for once in your life? Try it. You might like it."

"Asher..." She shook her head again, this time in admiration. Such a charmer, she thought, allowing her emotions to surface as she feasted on how he made her feel. Just looking at him made her all warm and gooey inside. Waking up in his arms had been sheer heaven. His lazy lovemaking had awakened in her a sense of well-being she hadn't known since childhood, before she learned that for every action there was a reaction and some weren't too pleasant. "We're too old and too wise to live for the day and not give one thought to tomorrow."

"As far as I can see, tomorrow holds no worries for me. This—you and me—can only get better."

Tess eased her hand from his. "I suppose I'm the kind of person who looks for gray clouds on a sunny day."

"What gray clouds do you see on the horizon, Tess?" His smile was pure sunshine.

"I see career complications," she admitted, looking away from his probing gaze. "How can we be lovers and competitors at the same time? I mean, assuming you want to continue this . . . this . . . well, this—"

"Affair?"

"Is that what it is?"

"By the time we get back to Kansas City, yes," he said with a slow grin. He sandwiched her hand between his and tickled her palm with his thumb, rubbing back and forth. The simple action was incredibly erotic and so absorbing she found it difficult to listen to him. "At this stage it's an encounter, by tonight it will be an interlude, by tomorrow we'll be an item and by the time we board the plane we'll be having an affair."

"I'm glad you fully understand the various phases and the jargon that goes along with them. I suppose such knowledge can only come from vast experience."

"From keen observation and research, my dear." He lifted her hand for a feather-light kiss. "One need not jump from a tall building to know about gravity."

She laughed at his scholarly tone. "I see, Professor. Getting back to my original point, if we continue this *affair* then we're bound to step on each other's toes. We're out to scoop each other, aren't we?"

"Competition is healthy. Our economy thrives on it."

"Our economy, yes, but competitors make strange bedfellows, don't you think?"

"I think we make great bedfellows. We might be strange, but that only sweetens the—"

"Hi, you two."

They both jumped, then laughed shakily when they were brought down to earth. Lenny looked from one to the other, a bemused expression on his face.

"Lenny!" Tess tugged her hand from Asher's and stood up to hug her friend. "I didn't see you in this morning's session."

"I was there, but it was hard to get your attention." His glance toward Asher said it all. "Anyway, we're all going to tour Hoover Dam after dinner and then catch the midnight show at the Sahara. You're coming along with us, right?"

"Uh . . . well . . ."

"No, sorry, we can't," Asher interjected smoothly. "We've made other plans."

"Other plans," Tess said, nodding and wondering what he had up his sleeve.

"Oh, well, I understand." Lenny kissed her cheek in a brotherly fashion. "Have fun."

"I will. Save us seats in the next session, will you?"

"Front row?"

"Front row," Tess said, patting Lenny's shoulder. "I want to grill the program director if I get a chance."

"You've got it." Lenny winked, gave a nod toward Asher and then left the restaurant along with several other people. The lunch crowd was thinning quickly.

"We should leave. I *do* want to question that head programmer," Tess said, gathering her belongings.

"Back to the salt mine," Asher said, sighing heavily.

"Why do I get the feeling your heart isn't in your work?"

"Work isn't what makes my heart go pitter-patter, sweetheart." He caught her wrist and ran the pad of his thumb across her lips. "You do."

"Asher, you're making me blush," she complained, feeling the evidence on her neck and face.

"So I see. Lovely."

"Where are we going tonight?"

"To heaven and back."

"No, really," she said, trying to get a straight answer out of him.

With a quick movement, he pulled her off balance so that she fell against him. His mouth claimed hers in a stinging kiss. "Really," he whispered.

"You're impossible," she said, regaining her equilibrium. "I never know what to expect from you."

"That's good."

"For you, maybe."

"For you, too." He pressed three fingertips to the small of her back, guiding her from the restaurant. "Knowing where you're going, how you're going to get there and what you're going to do once you're there is commendable, but it can also be boring. It's high time you got the rug pulled out from under you."

"Fine, so long as I don't get bruised in the process."

She marched to the front of the room with Asher on her heels. Lenny, as good as his word, removed his recorder and briefcase from the two chairs to his left, emptying them for Tess and Asher.

"Thanks," Tess whispered, then pushed all thoughts of affairs and heavenly, hellish kisses to the recesses of her mind. She took furious notes and checked often to make sure her tape recorder was working properly. All around her, other reporters did the same. Even Asher behaved himself.

During the question-and-answer period, the program director and his assistants ignored the front row, pointing to reporters behind Tess and her companions for questions. Just when she thought all was lost, the director's gaze lingered on her, shifted, then he raised his hand to point in her direction and her adrenaline soared. Finally!

"One more question," the director said. "Go ahead, Asher."

Tess wilted and glanced at the man who was her staunchest competition. He flipped through his notebook to locate a section he wanted to read from as part of his question, and Tess's competitive streak widened and overtook her kinder, gentler feelings toward him.

"You're on record as saying you don't like the prime-time soap operas," Tess said, verbally stampeding Asher. "Is that why you've given them such miserable time slots for next season? Are you hoping they'll do poorly and be canceled?"

Her peripheral vision alerted her to Asher's scathing glare and Lenny's smirk, but she kept her eyes glued to the man she'd questioned. He jerked at his collar in a gesture of discomfort, then cleared his throat and glanced at his assistants, who offered no help.

"Uh...no, of—of course not," he finally stammered. "I don't want any of our programs cancelled."

"So it was an accident that you moved both of them and pitted them against the number one and number two programs of last season."

"Are they?"

"So it was an accident?"

"Well, I wouldn't say an accident..."

"Then it was deliberate?" Tess persisted, the need to know churning in her like a tornado and blotting out everything else.

"No...I think they can gain respectable ratings."

"The producers say they'll be lucky to limp through midseason, but you're insisting you haven't sabotaged them because of your own dislike for that type of program?"

The object of her grilling narrowed his eyes, and his mouth thinned to a cold white line. "That's what I said. I expect them to do well and that's why I put them there. We need our best to combat our competitor's best, and I expect us to be victorious in those time slots."

"But neither was in the top ten last—"

"That's all the questions I'll take. Good day." With that, he turned sharply away from the throng of reporters and, flanked by his mute assistants, essayed a quick retreat.

"Wow," Lenny whispered. "Was he steamed. Way to go, Tess. I love it when we can get them off their prepared and rehearsed press releases and make them face the music. Good going."

"Thanks," Tess murmured, then turned to face her own music in the glowering expression of Asher Ames. "I was just dying to question him," she said, uncharacteristically meek. "You understand."

"No, I don't. Since when is your name Asher? You *did* hear him call on me by name, didn't you?" he demanded.

"Yes," she said, drawing out the word. "But you didn't jump right in, so I—"

"So you did. Have you ever heard of journalistic integrity?"

"Yes, but that has nothing to do with this," she said, stuffing her notebook and recorder into her large tote bag. "Let's go or we'll be late for the afternoon screenings."

"Not until you've apologized."

"For what?" she asked with a gasp. "Quit kidding around."

"I'm not. Your underhanded tactic was—"

"Hey, wait a minute, buster." She stood up to glare down at him. "There was nothing underhanded about what I did. It was just good, aggressive questioning."

"Oh, please," he said with a moan and rose up to face her. "You knifed me in the back."

"Give me a break," she pleaded, incensed by his self-righteousness. "*I'm* not the sneak, Ames, *you* are. I don't make dates with you and then tiptoe behind your back and snare interviews while you're waiting for me to show up!"

"I explained that last night. . . ."

"Right, so now you listen to *my* explanation." She rose on tiptoe to align her nose with his. "Unlike you, when *I* compete with you *I* do it right under your nose, not behind your back, which is *your* brand of journalistic integrity," she said, sneering the last two words. His anger made his eyes look like liquid smoke. Tess sought the exit without waiting for a retort she knew would singe, if not burn her to a crisp. But as she reached the exit, she heard him say, "Touché." When she glanced over her shoulder, he slanted an arm across his middle and executed a chivalrous bow.

"You've won the battle," he said. "But not the war."

7

"HEAVEN," Tess said, staring through the taxi windshield at the red neon lights spelling out the word against a magnificent sunset. "*This* is heaven?"

Asher leaned forward to press a twenty into the taxi driver's hand. "Remember, I told you I'd take you to heaven and back—"

"Yes, but—"

"And I know this isn't exactly what you expected—"

"Right again," Tess interrupted, in no hurry to leave the taxi and approach the four house trailers stuck together to make an L-shaped building. "Somehow I thought you were being poetic."

"Trust me," Asher said, patting her arm reassuringly. "You're going to like this."

"Asher, please tell me Heaven isn't a cathouse."

"Best one around," the taxi driver said, grinning back at her. "I've had fares from all over the world who've come here just to go to Heaven. It's all legal here, don't you know. All you need is a license."

She fashioned a sickly smile. "Lucky for me I don't have one. I want to go back to the hotel."

"No." Asher reached past her and opened the door. "We're expected. Don't be rude."

"Rude? You've taken me to a brothel and you're calling *me* rude?"

"Out, Maxwell. Out!" He gave her a none-too-gentle push. "Be a sport."

"What is that, the cathouse creed?" she complained, but unfolded herself from the back seat of the cab. Taking in her surroundings and finding them wanting, she propped her hands at her hips and hoped her mighty frown relayed her displeasure. "After a long day of screenings and interviews this is *not* my idea of a perfect nightcap, Ames."

"Don't be so hasty to judge." He mirrored her stance, his wrists holding back the sides of his wheat-colored linen jacket. "Words are your business, I know, but you don't want to eat them if you can help it." He quirked an eyebrow and sent her a wink. "So chill out, baby cakes. You're going to *love* this."

She crossed her arms and sent what she hoped was a poisonous glare. "I thought we were going to eat dinner and relax."

"We are."

She shot a glance toward the blinking sign again. "Who's going to hire out, you or me?"

"Neither," he said, then puffed out a labored sigh. "Honestly, Maxie, do you *really* think I'd expect you to hire out?" He rolled his silvery eyes. "Get real."

"*You* get real. I'm tired," she said, ticking off her list one finger at a time, "and I'm hungry and I lost my sense of humor sometime after lunch and I don't expect to recover it here in the middle of the desert at a house of ill repute!"

He patted the air. "Take it easy." He motioned in the general direction of the trailer houses. "Dinner awaits."

"In Heaven?"

"Yes." He gathered a handful of her cotton sweater, impeding her progress toward the trailers. "Not in there. Over there."

Tess swung around to examine the double-wide trailer, a discreet distance from the brothel business. It was partly concealed by a natural fence of saguaro and blooming desert brush. A two-storey addition had been built on in back, constructed mostly of sun-shielding chocolate-brown glass. A walkway edged with sea-shells invited guests, but a knee-high, calligraphy-lettered sign detailed what kind of guests: Private Residence. No Trespassing. No Solicitors Please. Make Deliveries To Business Next Door.

"Who lives here?" she asked after reading the sign.

"Angel."

"Give me a break."

"No, really. Angel Segovia. She heads up Heaven."

"We're having dinner with a madam," Tess said, stopping short of the winding seashell-strewn walk. "Gee, my dream come true."

"She's an old friend, but she won't be joining us for dinner. She has a business to run." He took one of her hands and tucked it into the crook of his arm, then escorted her along the walkway and to the front door. He rang the bell, and a voice floated out to them from inside the house, telling them to wait a moment. Asher squeezed Tess's hand. "You're going to like Angel."

"I wish you'd told me about this before we left the hotel."

"Why, so you could back out?"

"Exactly."

"You're such a stick-in-the-mud." Then the door swung open, and Asher's face lit up with pure delight. "Angel!"

The woman was short and plump with a regal air about her that commanded instant respect. Draped from shoulders to toes in a gold-and-green caftan, she shimmered as she hugged Asher to her ample bosom. Her glossy black hair and brown-sugar complexion testified to her Hispanic heritage. Slightly past middle age, her face showed only a few signs of wear. Lines fanned from her almond-shaped eyes and were etched on either side of her lush red mouth, but they didn't detract from her beauty. They added to it. Her laughter, husky and robust, brought a smile to Tess. Angel stepped back to let them inside, and a cloud of expensive perfume wafted out to entice them.

"Welcome, welcome. It's so good to see you again, Ash," she said in a sultry alto voice. "And you've brought your lady. Hello, Tess. I'm Angel." She held out a hand heavy with rings and shook hands with Tess.

Tess admired the living room, cooled by two ceiling fans and decorated with wicker and climbing plants.

"Everything is ready for you two," Angel said. "I'll take you back there. I hate to appear rude, but it's going to be a busy night in Heaven with all the conventions in town. In fact, I think a few of your colleagues have made appointments this evening."

"Who?" Asher asked, but Angel waved a finger at him.

"Uh-uh-uh," she scolded. "We don't kiss and tell in Heaven. Come right this way," Angel said, wiggling her fingers and passing quickly through the living room, dining room and cozy den. "As you might recall, Ash, the suite is back here."

"The suite?" Tess whispered, but by that time she was inside it and didn't need an explanation.

The suite was the two-storey addition, its dark brown glass offering an uninterrupted view of the desert vista.

"Just in case you're the shy and retiring type who might worry about such things, we can see out, but no one can see in," Angel said. "Your dinner is over there. . . ." She waved toward an Oriental screen. "Table for two behind that. And the bedroom and added attractions are upstairs." Holding out her arms so that her caftan sleeves resembled wings, she made a slow circle. "The fireplace is crackling, the wine has breathed and the water is just the right temperature, so enjoy."

At the mention of a bedroom, Tess looked sharply at Asher, but he pointedly ignored her, keeping his attention riveted on Angel. He embraced their hostess, closing his eyes as he received her answering hug.

"You're a treasure, Angel."

"That's what all the men say," she said, laughing. "Well, I should get to work. It was nice meeting you,

Tess," Angel said, already retracing her steps toward the front of the trailer. "If you're so inclined, there are terry-cloth robes hanging on the back of the bathroom door upstairs." Then the door to the suite closed behind her to cut them off from the rest of the house.

Tess turned to regard Asher's happy grin. "So, let me sort this out. You paid her for a dinner for two and a bed upstairs."

"Something like that."

"We could have stayed at the hotel and done the same thing, except our newspapers would have picked up the tab."

He regarded her for a few moments before disappointment became evident in the droop of his mouth. "How unromantic, Maxwell. We both need to get away from the hectic, dog-eat-dog atmosphere of the junket. This is a little pocket of heaven." He looked toward the quiet splendor of the desert and breathed deeply as if he could smell the outdoors. "I'd forgotten just how beautiful this place is."

"How did you know about it?" she asked. "Did you rent it before?"

He clasped his hands behind his back and went to stand before the smoked-glass wall to admire the splashy farewell of the sun. "I'm going to ignore the implication and answer the question. I met Angel a few years ago when I did a magazine article about legal prostitution. She told me about this special service reserved for lovers, and I filed it away for future reference. By the time we see that sun again, you'll be awfully glad I did."

Shrugging off any further objections to his plan, Tess removed her low heels. The salmon-colored carpet was deep pile and felt wonderful against the stinging soles of her feet. Might as well get comfortable, she thought, since it appeared she was going to be in Angel's special niche in Heaven until dawn.

"So, let's eat. I'm starving." Tess went toward the partitioned-off area.

"No, wait." Asher motioned her over to him, then draped an arm around her shoulders and looked toward the gold, purple and magenta horizon. "There's nothing quite as beautiful as a desert sunset."

"Ever been to Key West?"

"No, have you?"

She nodded. "The most beautiful sunsets in the world."

"Is this how it's going to be, Maxwell? Are you going to be obstinate all night long?"

"No." She leaned her head against his shoulder. "Sorry. I'm just tired and cranky. I'll be in a better mood once I've eaten."

"Okay, okay." He gripped her shoulders and marched her ahead of him to the partition. Rounding it, they both stopped to admire the table setting bathed in candlelight. "My, my. Isn't this nice?"

"Very romantic," Tess allowed, settling into the chair he held out for her. "Did this cost much?"

"I'm not going to tell you," he said, sitting across from her. Candlelight glowed in his eyes, reminding Tess of pewter.

"Why not?"

"Because you'll say it's too much money and I know good and well you're worth every cent." He grasped the neck of the wine bottle and examined the label. "Ah, perfect."

"You know, Ames, you didn't have to go to all this trouble. I would have slept with you tonight anyway."

His smile was fleeting as he removed the cork from the bottle. "You know, Maxwell, my objective isn't merely sex. I can get that next door and for less money." He poured the wine and his gaze lifted to hers. "We both got hot under the collar today, didn't we?"

"Oh, you mean that business about journalistic integrity?" Tess said, then dismissed it with a flick of her hand. She raised her glass and tapped it against his. "Here's to selective memories."

"Here, here." He took a drink, nodding his approval, then shook out the linen napkin and laid it across his lap. "Although the incident did illustrate our tendency to one-up each other."

"It's all in the game. That's what I've been trying to tell you, Ames. We're natural enemies."

"No." His eyes grew dark under lowered brows. "No," he repeated, giving a shake of his head. "We're not enemies. That, I won't accept, especially not after last night."

The mention of their lovemaking took the wind from her sails. He had kissed every pulse point; he knew her as no other man knew her. And she knew him; knew how his body hair thickened across his chest and below his navel, knew of the sickle-shaped scar on his left knee, knew that his flat nipples responded to the massage of her eager tongue.

He lifted a silver lid off the serving dish in the center of the table to reveal a seafood salad surrounded by crisp salted wafers.

"That certainly looks good," Tess said, grateful for the diversion. She leaned forward for a better view of the shrimp, salmon and tuna scattered among creamy macaroni and chunks of cheese and black olives. Asher revealed the contents of the side dish—oysters—and Tess's gaze snapped to his. A common thought arced between them, making Tess giggle. "Oysters," she said. "How corny."

"Do you think it's true . . . that they're an aphrodisiac?"

She smiled, her gaze dropping away because she couldn't look him in the eye when she answered, "I guess we'll soon find out."

"SO *THIS* IS WHAT made such a lasting impression on you," Tess said, having gained access to the second floor.

The bed was a thing of beauty, low to the floor and obviously custom-made—it was too narrow for a queen-size, but too large to be a double. There was no headboard, posters or canopy. In its spartan state, it invited and promised a firm mattress beneath its furry spread.

"Ta-daa!"

Looking toward Asher to see what he was trumpeting, her gaze collided with the hot tub and she stumbled backward, away from it.

"Oh, no."

"Oh, yes," Asher said, a lascivious glint in his eyes.

"You're not getting me into that thing."

Steam rose above the rim, curling in midair like a crooked finger. The faint sound of popping bubbles enticed her, and Tess went toward the tub. Glancing over the rim at the gently turbulent water and flower petals floating on its surface, she decided it looked an awful lot like a whirlpool. She retreated as the rich aroma of roses and spice lifted from the water.

Large ferns and potted trees circled it, lending an outdoor appeal. Track lighting pinpointed strategic spots such as the two steps against one side, a bowl of fresh fruit, a bucket of iced champagne and a basket overflowing with washclothes, towels, sponges and terry-cloth mitts. Positioned in the ceiling directly over the tub was a huge Casablanca fan that stirred the air and provided an orangy-golden light from the globe at its center.

"This is unreal," Tess said, laughing a little. "Now I know why Angel told us that nobody can see us from outside." She looked past the tub to the stunning beauty of the desert all around them. "It's like something out of an architectural magazine."

"Just think how wonderful it will feel."

She thought about it and felt herself blush again. "Ames, I told you. This . . . that—" She pointed to the tub. "Well, it's just not my style."

"Call me Asher. You should be on a first-name basis with a man you're going to get naked with in a hot tub."

"No," she said, laughing as he approached with a predatory gait. "No!" Stiff-armed, she held him off. "Tell you what . . . let's cut to the chase and go to bed."

"And waste that hot tub? No way." He batted aside her hand, and his mouth settled comfortably on hers in a persuasive kiss. "Trust me. You'll love it."

"It's too *contrived*. It's too hippie, and I'm a yuppie."

"You're a yuppie?" he scoffed. "Right, and I'm a guppy."

"A guppy? What's that?"

"Someone who loves water . . . hot, bubbling water in a big old wooden tub."

"Asher!" She giggled, his playfulness and tickling mouth getting the best of her. Angling her neck away from his nibbling mouth, she captured his silvery gaze. "You go first."

"Promise you'll go second?"

"Well . . ."

"Promise," he repeated.

"Okay, I promise."

He gripped her wrists and brought her hands up to inspect her crossed fingers.

"You know me too well," Tess said, uncrossing her fingers. "That scares me more than the idea of you and me in that hot tub."

"Why are you scared?"

"This—" She encompassed the whole room with a wave of her hand "—is so decadent. I guess I'm feeling insecure. Kind of out of my element."

"Any other woman would be feeling pampered."

She nodded, realizing the error of her ways. "Okay. I promise to jump in right after you."

He glanced down at her stockinged feet. Tess laughed and pushed him toward the tub.

"I couldn't cross my toes if my life depended on it. Get in the tub, guppy."

"I have to undress first, you know," he said, standing beside the tub, unaware of the breathtaking picture he presented, with the twilight desert spreading out behind him. "You can watch, if you want."

"Gee, thanks." She figured he thought she'd turn her back, seized by modesty, so she forced herself to stare straight at him. It wasn't any great sacrifice. She folded her arms negligently against her chest, where her heart leaped with anticipation. "Don't mind if I do."

He shrugged, making her wonder if he was really as cool and nonchalant as he appeared, then he began to strip. Striptease, that is. Buttons escaped buttonholes, one at a time, down his chest. The stylish knit tie of burned orange unfurled and snaked to the floor at his feet where empty shoes and crumpled socks soon joined it. The belt came next, then the mocha trousers. He inched them down his legs slowly, mischievously, then kicked them away.

Tess worked hard at not showing her avid interest. She hadn't forgotten how gorgeous he was, but seeing him standing in the golden light, clad only in a pair of tight jockey shorts, was almost more than she could bear. Every sense cried for fulfillment. Every nerve sprang to life within her. A burning began in her belly and then spread lower. Amber spilled over his inky hair and across his shoulders, making his dark skin glow. She wanted to slip her fingers through the mat on his chest and then slide her hand down to—

"Moment of truth," he said, breaking into her erotic thoughts. "Ready?"

"Ready or not," Tess said, matching his grin. "Here I come." Had that husky voice come from her? Tess drew in a shaky breath and closed the distance between them. She lifted her face for his kiss then slid her fingers inside the elastic band riding his hips. His breathing shortened and a patina of perspiration made his skin glisten. Tess peeled the jockeys down his lean, sinewy legs and let him step out of them. She rose up to meet his swooping mouth.

Her arms circled him and her hands settled on his firm buttocks. She tore her mouth from his to gather in needed air and pressed her face into the curve of his neck. Through a haze of passion she realized he was undressing her, and she gave herself up to him. The cherry-red sweater was swept up and over her head. He unbuttoned her white shirt, his fingers trembling, and pushed it off her shoulders, down her arms, sent it fluttering like a huge bird across the room. Her slacks gave him the most trouble, and he cursed under his breath when he couldn't get rid of them fast enough to suit him.

Laughing lightly at his impatience, Tess pushed him away and finished undressing in a flurry, then she returned to his waiting arms. The friction of his skin against hers was all she needed to float again in that hazy cloud of desire. She kissed him, openmouthed, her tongue searching his out. But her hunger was meager compared to his.

His hands roamed her back and hips then swept up to frame her face. He tipped her head sideways so that his mouth could slant more completely upon hers and his tongue could enter and exit until she was swimming in a hot tide of longing. Sweeping her into his arms, he carried her up the steps and down into the tub of erotic pleasure.

The water was warm. Its surface bubbled gently, just enough to make sailing ships of the rose petals. The smell of blooming things filled her head, and Asher filled her hands with his satiny-skinned erection.

"Touch me, hold me," he whispered fiercely between drowning kisses.

Sitting on the smooth bench with the water lapping around her waist, Tess stroked him, stoking his inner fire. He touched her tight nipples with fingers that trembled, and she flung her head back, shaken by the lightning flash of passion that simple caress triggered within her. When he took one nipple into his mouth, Tess wondered if her sizzling feelings were too much for a mere mortal to endure.

"Asher, Asher." She plowed her fingers through his damp hair and then across his wet shoulders. Her legs lifted, almost of their own accord, and she hooked her heels at the back of his muscled thighs.

"I can never get close enough to you...never can get enough of you," he murmured, kissing her waiting mouth again as he plunged into her.

The joining was an experience beyond pleasure, far and away better than passion. It was soulful, celestial, otherworldly. Stars swam overhead, swirling in a giddy dance, then Tess closed her eyes and concentrated solely on the slip and slide of Asher as he filled her again and again, faster and faster. Each burning stroke took something away and then gave it back to her tenfold.

"To heaven and back," he whispered hoarsely, and she took his face in hand and tattooed his lips with quick, hard kisses. "Do you want me?" he asked when the onslaught slowed.

"Yes, now...now, please now."

He complied immediately, and his final thrust stilled her raging emotions for a shattering silent second before everything seemed to break loose.

Sounds of wonder and ecstasy escaped him. Hoarse, guttural, a distinctly masculine paean. Tess ran her thumbs lovingly along his sleek brows, his forehead, his prominent cheekbones.

I worship him, she thought jolted by the sincerity of her emotion. She wanted only to pleasure him and to know the pleasure of him. Perhaps this was the love she'd waited for, dreamed of, secretly prayed for night after night. . . .

"I'm wiped out," he said between panting breaths, then he moved and stretched, severing the linking chain of flesh. "That was so intense I'm not sure I can recover fully."

She laughed and pushed his hair off his forehead. The strands curling around her fingers, black and shot through with silver, held her gaze for a few moments. She glanced up, finding the same colors in the sky.

"Look," she said, tipping back his head. "We're being swallowed by stars."

He floated on his back, stretching out away from her. Stars were everywhere, virtually engulfing them. He ducked under the water and came up in a shower of glistening drops. Tess laughed lazily and straightened her legs until she could flatten her feet against his firm stomach. She nudged him with her toes and got a grin from him.

Enclosing one foot in his hands, he lifted it to suck each toe, his thumbs circling in a gentle massage. Tess sighed and flung her arms behind her along the rim of the tub. She followed his gaze to her breasts, which floated like twin moons in the water.

"You're beautiful," Asher said, continuing his massage on her other foot.

Her free foot slid between his legs, and she felt the muscles in his thighs flex. Her toes began a massage of their own, bringing life to his member.

"Now that surprises me," he said, looking down at himself and shaking his head in rapt amazement. "I thought I was too old for that kind of action. You know, we're told that with age comes a slower recovery time."

"Honey, you've just met your match, that's all."

He studied her sexy, confident smile. "My thoughts exactly."

Unnerved by his sudden dead seriousness, she looked away. Her heart hammered in her chest, making her dizzy. She closed her eyes and took a head-clearing breath. When she opened her eyes again, she was struck once more by the beauty around them.

"Wonder what kind of people rent this place?"

"People like us, I guess. People who need to get away from the world and find a new world in each other's arms."

"Why, Asher Ames," she said, letting her gaze slip from the stars to the sparkle in his gray eyes. "You're a poet."

"If I am, then you're my inspiration." He covered the space between them in one fluid motion. Bracketing her hips with his arms, his upper body sliding against hers, he kissed her hard. "I've never felt like this before with anyone else. I want you to know that."

"Be careful." She pressed her fingertips to his lips. "I'm going to remember every little thing you say tonight. I'll cherish every word, every gesture, every nuance."

"That's the idea, sweetheart. Now kiss me. Swallow me up. Make me yours."

She brought his mouth to hers and smiled against his smile. She outlined his lips with the tip of her tongue, then tested the seam of his mouth. His lips parted to take hers. His arms came around her. His body joined hers again in a hot rush of excitement and the world slipped away. Far, far away.

WRAPPED IN WHITE terry-cloth robes, Tess and Asher lay sprawled on the bed, both gazing up at the moon and its tiny companions. Asher rocked Tess in his arms, dropping a kiss now and then on the tip of her nose or upon her flushed cheek.

Snug and warm against him, Tess reached blindly for the bowl of fruit, found it and plucked out another strawberry. She popped it into her mouth.

"What time is it?" she asked.

"Who cares?"

"I want to know how much time we have left."

"The rest of our lives, that's how much."

"Oh," Tess sighed. "If only that were true."

"Why isn't it?"

"Because we have to get back to the hotel soon, and day after tomorrow we'll be heading back to Missouri." That thought filled her with such dread she had to choke down the last bite of strawberry.

Asher slipped out from under her and turned onto his belly so he could look her squarely in the face. "Are you still quoting doom and gloom? After what we've just shared? After the hot tub and this bed? You *still* think we can't scale the heights?"

"The heights we can scale," she said. "It's the valleys that have me worried. Have you forgotten how we've treated each other in the name of the 'big story,'" she said, making quotation marks with her forefingers. "You think we'll make nicey-nice once we're back in the work arena?"

"Why not?"

She sighed. "There's more to this than you know." Glancing at him, she saw he was waiting for her to clear the air. She wondered where to begin, then decided to open up to him fully and damn the consequences. "You see, I applied for your job and I kind of had it in the bag until you threw your hat into the ring." She glanced at him again, expecting shock, but his expression remained unchanged. He was still waiting. "I tell you this so you'll see how you and I keep bumping into each other, bruising each other without really meaning to. I wanted that job—your job—and when you got the nod, it only pointed out once again that you're better at this than I am—or *perceived* to be better," she added quickly when he opened his mouth to protest.

Asher continued to stare at her while he wrestled with his own urge to explain. He thought about telling her that he'd known she had applied for the job he now had, but something told him to keep quiet. A confession might add insult to injury. It might bruise her even more deeply, and he didn't want to hurt her. He never, ever wanted that. So he pressed his lips together and lifted one hand to cradle the side of her face. Her smile, sweetly angelic, made his heart constrict and then swell with every wondrous emotion known to man.

"So is there hope, Dr. True Love?" she asked, her eyes brimming with sentimental tears.

"There is always hope." He tugged the knot from the belt at her waist. "We don't have to roll over and play dead and we don't have to bulldoze each other. We'll find a happy medium."

"Ash, do you think we can? Do you *really*?"

"Yes, if we try. Don't you?"

She studied his hopeful expression and wanted to kiss him until he cried for mercy. "I think you're as cute as a button, that's what I think."

"No, no," he said, shaking his head and chuckling good-naturedly. "I'm not cute. I'm one hot, handsome, hunky hombre."

"Oh, I see." She snuggled down and he squirmed upward until their mouths met in a stirring kiss.

"Don't you think we're great together?" he murmured against her shoulder, breathing in her aroma.

"Yes, but I also think rival newspaper reporters having an affair sounds like the premise for a situation comedy, but it doesn't play in real life."

"Come here, you." He tucked one hand between her back and the mattress and opened her robe with the other. "I'll show you real life." With a growl, he nuzzled the patch of skin between her breasts and tickled with his tongue.

Tess released a gale of laughter that melted into giggles and then tapered off into a moan as his tongue grazed one nipple and then his mouth fastened on the other. Taking his time, he teased it into a flushed, throbbing peak. His tongue left a trail as he moved lower until he located that nugget of flesh that made her jerk convulsively and gasp out his name. He looked up. His eyes were dark; hers were darker.

"Is it real life or an imitation?" he asked with a taunting smile.

"It's real," Tess said on a long sigh, then she laced her fingers at the back of his head and pressed him into service.

8

"DID YOU LEAVE YOUR CAR here or can I give you a lift?" Asher asked as he stood beside Tess and watched the luggage carousel go around and around.

"My car's in the long-term parking lot."

"Mine, too."

"Wonder where our luggage is?" Tess asked, anxious to be home now that she was on Kansas City soil.

"It's coming."

She glanced sideways at Asher. He looked bored, tired, impatient. "Well, here we are. Back to the salt mines tomorrow."

"Yeah," he said on a long sigh. "But it was nice while it lasted. I know I'll never forget this particular junket." He slid her a sidelong glance, and his grin talked dirty to her.

She blushed and nudged him with her shoulder. "Stop that."

"What?" he asked, as innocent as a choirboy.

"You know what."

"What did I say to make you turn red in the face?"

"It's not what you said *aloud*. That grin of yours and those eyes do most of your talking for you."

He chuckled and looked to the fluttering strips covering the luggage chute. A garment bag slipped out like a big brown tongue. "Here they come," he announced, and the people around them elbowed and angled for better positions. "What color?" he asked, turning halfway around to address Tess.

"Silver. It's metal and it's got a *T* of orange tape on each side."

He eyed her. "You take traveling seriously, don't you?"

"My uncle is a luggage handler in Dallas. He bought the luggage for me and suggested the initial trick." She pointed. "There's mine!"

He whipped his head around and used the broad wedge of his shoulders to insert himself among the other luggage grabbers. He snagged the silver suitcase and swung it off and around to Tess.

"Thanks, sweetie."

The endearment fell from her lips as naturally as rain falls from gray clouds. Asher had started to turn back to the carousel, but her whispered love word brought his attention to her again. He looked surprised for an instant and so did she, then he grinned from ear to ear as if she'd given him the best present possible.

"You're welcome, sweetheart."

Even though it was calculated, the feeling he put behind the endearment was genuine, and it made Tess's heart soar into her throat. She blinked as tears shimmered in her eyes. In that instant she loved him with every fiber of her being. From the corner of her eye she saw a black suit-carrier slide past, and she recognized it as his. She pointed, his gaze followed and the moments of intimacy ended.

"Oh, damn," he said, making a grab for his luggage and missing it. "Sir, could you snag that for me, please?" he asked a balding man down the way. "Thanks."

"No problem," the man said, lifting the suit-carrier and holding it out to Asher.

Asher took it and led the way through the crowd to the automatic doors. He went through first, then waited for Tess to catch up.

"So where's your car?" he asked, taking her case from her.

"That way," she said, motioning in the general direction.

"Mine, too."

"I can carry my case," she said.

"So can I." He smiled and set off. She took two steps to his one.

It was windy, blowing topsoil and dried grass into Tess's eyes. She fought her skirt to keep it from flying up over her head and giving everyone a free show. Asher dipped his chin and forged ahead. He nodded when she pointed out her car.

"Mine is a row over," he said, setting her luggage down while she located her keys and unlocked the door. He put the case into the back seat for her, then caught her by the shoulders and kissed her. "Are we going to spend the night together?"

"Tonight?"

"Yes," he said, laughing.

"I don't know. I've got a lot of catching up to to."

"And you're tired," he tacked on, running his thumbs under her eyes where shadows gathered. "I can see you are. Okay, then call me later before you go to bed, and I'll tell you what I'd be doing to you if you weren't so tired."

She pressed her mouth to his. "You're so naughty."

"And you love it."

Nodding, she nudged his mouth with hers. "And I love it. Go on." She gave him a push. "I'll call you after I've unpacked and taken a bath."

"Call me while you're in the tub," he suggested, his eyebrows doing push-ups. "And use your powers of description to tell me what you see."

"Will you get out of here," she said, laughing and dodging his moist mouth. He got another kiss in before he sauntered away.

Watching him, Tess thought he had the sexiest damn walk she'd ever seen.

"STAHLMAN'S ATTEMPT AT directing slapstick makes the viewer want to slap him and stick him in a corner until he learns the difference between what's funny and what's asinine."

Asher tossed the newspaper into the trash can beside his desk and released a hiss.

"Something wrong?" Skip asked.

Looking across his cluttered desk, Asher shook his head at his assistant.

"Did Maxwell scoop us on something?" Skip persisted.

"No, nothing like that." Asher ran a hand down his face and told himself he was getting hot under the collar for no good reason. "We just don't see eye to eye on the new Stahlman film."

"Let me guess. She hated it."

"You got it, slick." His neck grew red again, scorching his collar. "Can you believe it? I laughed so hard my stomach muscles hurt the next day, and she says there's not one funny scene in the whole movie."

He shook his head again, thinking how the difference in their thinking on the film mirrored the discord that had existed between them since their return from Las Vegas two weeks ago. The competition had renewed with a vengeance when the newspaper had printed his interview with an illustrious actress, who had granted only three interviews in the past ten years, one being Asher's. The exchange had taken place during the networks' junket while Tess had paced in her hotel room and waited for him. A wire service had picked up Asher's story, and he'd even sold it to a major magazine. The news had been taken by Tess with equal parts of loving pride and grudging envy. With a tight smile, she'd told him she'd even the score some day, and he had no reason to doubt her.

By night they were one, but the days were testing them. He knew it. She knew it. The only thing they didn't know was how to find a balance. That happy medium he'd talked about in Heaven was about as easy to find as a film they both liked.

"There's no accounting for taste," Skip said, tugging Asher back to the most current difference of opinion. "I thought it was funny, too. Maxwell's outnumbered."

Asher bent over the story he'd been editing, but his mind returned to Tess's bedroom two nights ago when even their lovemaking had been tainted by preoccupation. His sense that Tess hadn't been all there had been confirmed when, rocked in his arms, she'd revealed that she'd sent her résumé off to several papers outside Kansas City. The news had at once irritated him—had she been thinking of work while he'd been making love to her?—and worried him. If job offers came from outside the city, she'd move and he'd lose her again. But he'd kept quiet, chained by an attack of self-doubt that had nagged him since then.

The doubt poisoned everything, and he even wondered if her passion for him had waned. Maybe he was a fool to think she'd place him and his love above any career considerations.

Day after day their differences were strung out on lines of type like so much laundry. She praised a miniseries, and he found it wanting. He applauded a midseason television replacement, and she thumbed her nose at it. She drooled over a star-making vehicle released by a minor film company, and he noted the slight plot, spotty direction and hokey ending of the film.

So far the only thing they'd agreed on in their respective entertainment sections was the cancellation of
the three least-watched programs on the television
schedule. Hardly the stuff for celebration.

But the differences were in taste and could be ironed
out, he thought, *if* she stayed close. If she moved to
some far-off corner, how could he keep the fires burning? Seeing her a weekend every so often held no appeal for him. He had to find a way to keep her in Kansas
City. Some kind of great job . . . something tailored to
her skills . . .

"Where are you going?" Skip asked.

"What?" Asher was already on his feet and turning
away. "Oh . . . I've got to see Harry about something.
Be back in a few minutes." He straightened his tie and
rolled down his shirtsleeves as he crossed the newsroom
to the bank of editorial offices. It's a long shot, he told
himself as his flash of inspiration took shape and depth
in his mind. First he'd sell Harry Caper on the idea, and
then he'd convince Tess that he had her best interests at
heart.

"THE MAN'S TASTE is all in his mouth," Tess said, tossing aside the newspaper. She'd just read Asher's latest
review of a film over the phone to Dana. She'd found
the movie tedious and he'd praised it to high heaven.
"Oh, yes," she said as an afterthought. "He also has ex-
cellent taste in women." Her humorous aside brought
a smile to her but a groan from Dana.

"I was kidding, Dana."

"Don't kid around with a danger like Asher Ames," Dana advised. "Now listen, I think you should get away from him for a while. Why don't you visit me this weekend?"

"I just recovered from Las Vegas, Dana. Another trip so soon . . ."

"You need some breathing room. Once you're clear of Asher's influence, you'll see that you need to get rid of him before this whole thing turns ugly."

"Who says it will?"

"The voice of experience."

"I'll think about it. Thanks for the invitation."

"Say you'll come," Dana insisted.

"Oh, all right. We haven't seen each other since Christmas."

"I know."

"I'll get a ticket for Friday night."

"Great! We'll have a ball. I promise."

"Don't plan anything elaborate. I just wish to visit you, not be entertained."

"Yes, ma'am. Oh, shoot. I've got to go. My timer just went off."

"What timer?"

"Oven. I'm baking bread."

"Bread?" Tess said, amazed. "You're so domestic, Dana. You should get out more, kiddo. You know, you can buy perfectly good bread at the grocery these days, and it's even sliced!"

"But you don't know what they've put in that stuff, do you? I *know* what goes into *my* bread."

"Right," Tess said, realizing this was a lost cause. "Go see to your bread. Bye."

"See you Friday night. I'll pick you up at the airport."

"Okay," Tess said, and returned the receiver to its cradle.

Getting up from the easy chair in the corner of her living room, Tess gathered the newspapers scattered across the floor and stuffed them into a trash bin under the kitchen sink. So much for journalism, she thought with a self-deprecating smirk. Hours of selecting the right word, constructing the correct sentence and tying one paragraph to the next resulted in a quick reading by subscribers and then a toss into the trash can. Hers was throwaway prose in a throwaway society.

Settling into the overstuffed chair again, she brought her legs up and wrapped her arms around them. Her gaze came to rest on the shelf where she kept her film library, and she recalled that, aside from the recognized classics, Asher had found only one he termed as "better than average." It had become apparent that she favored low-budget, romantic comedies while he worshipped at the altar of the so-called epic films, those money-eating monstrosities most often praised for their cinematography, costumes and egocentric direction than for their scripts or the caliber of the acting.

More and more lately, she'd begun to doubt the heaven they'd discovered in Las Vegas. Had it all been a fluke? Could two people in such complete disagreement agree on a future together? Maybe Dana was right. Maybe she and Asher were running out of gas.

The worries vibrated in her head, making it feel like a hive of swarming bees. Returning from Las Vegas, they'd both been swamped with work. The other night, they'd set aside the evening to cuddle in bed and watch a movie, but selecting one they both liked had been an exercise in head butting. They'd finally settled on a golden-oldie musical and had made love during the last half of it, but Tess had been left feeling guilty since she hadn't given Asher her all that night.

She'd decided that her career in Kansas City was at a standstill, and she'd sent out her résumés. Her mind had been full of the changes that act might bring to her life, and she hadn't been able to remain in the moment with Asher. Worse, she knew he'd felt her partial absence.

It pained her to think of leaving Kansas City, especially now that the man of her dreams lived here, too, and she'd finally told Asher of her decision to look for better work. His silent acceptance told her more than she'd ever wanted to know about the quality of his feelings for her.

"Not one, lousy, discouraging word," she murmured, her hands tightened into fists of outrage. "Not one! The very least he could have done was to tell me he'd hate to see me sail off into the wild blue yonder. He just turned over and fell asleep."

Which once again underlined their incompatibility, she told herself, wincing at the sting of it. He couldn't say he hadn't been warned. Being right was the pits, she thought, her throat tightening, burning.

Leaning back her head, she closed her eyes, saw him, and her heart smiled. If only Las Vegas could have lasted forever. The minute they'd set foot in Kansas City, they'd returned to their respective corners, put on the gloves and had come out fighting.

Speaking of which . . . She grinned wickedly as her thoughts zapped her to the interview she'd wrangled from a bigger-than-big ballet star turned actor, who was scheduled to appear in a Kansas City showcase in a couple of days. From the telephone conversation with the Russian-born dancer, she'd gleaned that Asher had already interviewed him and had made him promise not to grant other interviews until he arrived in Kansas City.

That's when she'd turned on the charm and had dropped enough names to get the dancer's attention. Impressing him with her knowledge of ballet and his part in it, she'd convinced him to break his silly little promise to that other reporter and run off at the mouth. It had been a great interview, and she'd written an article that went beyond the usual newspaper piece. She'd gone the distance by interviewing his first American ballet partner and his first American ballet choreographer. Her article, published that afternoon and only hours old, was insightful and, if she did say so herself, technically brilliant. Before leaving the office, Jess had informed her that the wire service had picked it up.

"Take that, Ames," she whispered, but her burst of satisfaction had the life span of a falling star. "Oh, Ash," she said, her voice dipping to a purr of dissatisfaction. How could they be lovers and fighters at the same time? Even while she ached to feel him inside her, she waited to throw the knockout punch.

The abrupt rapping at her apartment door made her heart lurch into her throat.

"Wh-who is it?" she called out.

"Ames."

Trepidation threaded through her at the sound of his growling voice and the use of his last name. She left the chair and opened the door. He strode in, head down, brows lowered over smoldering gray eyes. She felt as if she'd just let a storm cloud into her apartment, and she had no doubt once he whirled about to face her that he was there to rain on her parade.

"How did you get this interview?" he asked, displaying the entertainment page of the afternoon newspaper. Her article on the ballet star was stretched across the top. "I interviewed this guy and he promised me an exclusive."

"He changed his mind," Tess said, shrugging aside the incident but gloating inside. "Happens all the time."

"I suppose this gave you a lot of satisfaction," he said, sneering at her.

"Yes, yes it did," she agreed, standing hip cocked in front of the sliding glass doors where the late-afternoon sun spread heat and slanting bars of light. "As much satisfaction as you would have had if your interview had been published before mine. If you think I'm going to apologize for stealing your thunder, Asher, then you've come to the wrong cloud bank."

He winced at her lame metaphor, but it did take some of the ill wind from him. "I wonder if you'd have worked so damned hard on this piece if you hadn't somehow discovered I was writing on the same subject and thought I had an exclusive."

"What difference does it make?" She crossed her arms, gathering the front of her too-large man's shirt into folds.

"Not much to me, but it does to you. Did you do the article for your readers or just to get even with me?" He flung the newspaper onto her couch, fighting against an urge to wound her with words and losing the skirmish. "What would you do without me, Maxwell?"

"It's business. I was a good reporter before you came to town, Asher, so don't flatter yourself." That he'd take her skills and attribute them to himself indirectly made her shrink from him. "Dana's right. You put yourself above everyone."

"How did Dana get into this?"

"I just talked to her."

"About me?"

"Among other things."

"If you want to hear someone bad-mouth me, I can give you some local numbers and save you those long-distance charges."

She curled into the chair again, making herself as small a target as possible. "If you're going to continue being hateful, you can leave."

"I don't mean to. . . ." He stopped himself, realizing he was building a gigantic lie. "No, I *did* mean to make you bleed a little. But, honestly, Tess, didn't you think about my reaction all the time you were writing that interview? Didn't you?" he demanded, bending at the waist to drill her eyes with his.

"Did you think of *my* reaction when you were interviewing that woman at the hotel while—"

"Aha!" He straightened and held one finger aloft. "So that *was* uppermost in your mind when you screwed up my exclusive."

"I didn't say that."

"That's what I heard."

"Then you need your hearing checked."

"You need to put aside your petty jealousies, sweetheart."

"You need to leave before I slap your face."

He stared at her stony expression and relented. "This is about as productive as a bed full of eunuchs." He turned and strode toward the door. A big part of her wanted her to call him back, but she didn't.

Outside Tess's apartment, Asher stared at the apartment number tacked to the door and struggled with his inner demons. He wanted to go back inside and start all over, but the devil in him goaded him from her apartment and outside to his parked car.

Sitting in the low-slung sports car, he tapped out a nervous percussion number against the steering wheel with his forefingers and thumbs while he examined his own faults instead of focusing on hers. Strangely, the faults blurred, hers into his, his into hers. They were the same, just dressed up in different clothing. It all boiled down to survival in the newspaper arena. She was voraciously competing against him while he was merely responding with the knee-jerk reaction of a seasoned reporter. When a journalist was scooped, he scooped back at the earliest opportunity to satisfy himself and appease his disgruntled bosses. The only difference was he happened to be falling in love with his competitor.

Bad form, my man, he thought to himself with a grim smile. Bad form, indeed.

Maybe she was right, he mused. Maybe it was impossible to keep their social life on an even keel while they slugged it out during working hours.

"No." The word blasted from the very heart of him. He refused to use the nature of their work as an excuse for their bad behavior toward each other. In retrospect, he knew he shouldn't have dropped in on her with all the geniality of a bee-stung bear. He should have calmed down first, he thought, resting his forehead against his hands on the leather-wrapped steering wheel.

He switched on the radio, found an instrumental and let it soothe him. It had been a hellacious week, topped off by Tess's surprise interview with a source he thought he had all to himself. His article was written and stored in the computer, ready to be printed the very next morning, but Tess had doused it, taken away its fire.

"It'd be easier if she weren't so damned talented," he muttered, then laughed at his unkindness. "That's what you're so angry about, Ames. Give her an inch and she takes a mile."

Lifting his head, he looked at her apartment building and decided he should be saying these things to *her* instead of himself, so he left his car and retraced his steps.

Asher knocked, then buzzed, but she didn't answer. "Tess, come on and open the door. I promise to be on my best behavior. I was a chump before. Tess?" He listened, but heard no sound from within.

Dispirited, he turned away, surprised she refused to confront him again. Then he remembered seeing a basket of clothes sitting on the coffee table. Acting on intuition, he skipped down two flights of stairs to the basement laundry. Rounding the corner, he heard the sloshing of a loaded washer and he broke into a grin.

Tess sat on an idle washer, magazine draped across her jean-clad lap, one hand holding a banana and the other a can of soda pop. She looked up as he entered the laundry room and then frowned.

"I thought you were all washed up," she said, dry wit intact.

"You're clever," he said, wagging a finger at her and finding her so cute he wanted to embrace her and give her a smacking kiss. But after his last performance, he knew she'd not take too kindly to such a display, so he

settled for a quick bite of her banana. She yelped a protest and whipped the rest of it behind her back.
"Wouldn't it be nice if our life was a cassette tape?" he
asked, keeping her off balance.

"No," she said, setting the can of pop and magazine
to one side.

"We could erase the past half hour and tape something over it," he elaborated. "Something nicer. Something more adult."

She took a bite of banana, then hid it from him again.

"I apologize for my conduct," Asher said. "I
shouldn't have barged in, bent on destruction. You're
right, I was sore because you bested me, but you have
to agree with me about your ulterior motive."

"I don't have to agree with you about anything."

"Which is the crux of our problem." He propped his
hands at either side of her knees to box her in. "No
matter what it takes and no matter how much it hurts,
you're going to show me up. Not for the good of your
newspaper or for the edification of your readership, but
for your own ego. Isn't that about it, Tess?"

She chewed the banana to pulp before she swallowed it with difficulty. "I should hope I'd do the same
to your predecessor, Ash. In fact, I did. I beat his drum
every chance I got, which was often."

"I can see we're not going to see eye to eye on this."

"That surprises you?"

"It disappoints me." He hung his head, wondering
which way to go from here.

Seeing him thus, head bowed and shoulders rounded, pity squirmed into her heart. Tess took his whisker-stubbled chin in hand and lifted his head. "When you're second best, you have to try harder. I don't expect you to understand that, being top dog as you are."

"I'm hardly that. This is Kansas City, not Los Angeles or New York."

"No, but you're top dog in this pound." She rested her forehead against his. "Don't bite my head off for trying to claw my way up to your level, Asher. Please, don't do that."

"I don't mean to . . . and I don't think of you as below me in any way, shape or form."

"Ash, it's all part of the game." She dropped her hand from his chin, pushed the rest of the banana into his hand and leaned back on stiff arms. "Maybe I can't write as well as you and maybe I don't have your varied background in reporting, but those aren't the only qualifications of a good reporter. What I might lack in technique, I make up for in hustle."

Asher finished the banana and went to drop the peel into a metal container near the entrance. His footfalls echoed off the concrete walls and ceiling. Every sound was amplified, making the little things all that much more important.

"I never said I wrote better than you," he said, weighing her words. In profile she was near perfect, he thought as his eyes traced the short bridge of her nose put those around us under conviction. And this may very well lead to some form of persecution.

I had firsthand experience with this in junior high. While attending a public school, I was often challenged about my beliefs. As I took a stand for my faith, it earned me the nickname "Reverend Allen." A few guys even challenged me to a fight after school just to see if Christians were "sissies" or "tough guys." Robert Crawford, a six-foot, two-inch African-American with a nice switchblade, intervened before things got nasty. Robert later told me that he stood up for me because he respected my courage.

During more than two decades in the ministry, I have also felt the sting of persecution for my willingness to stand up for the truth. After John Lennon's murder in December, 1980, I wrote a letter to the editor of a local newspaper. I complained about all the hoopla surrounding the death of a man who once dared to say of the Beatles, "We are more popular than Jesus Christ." I simply "told the truth" about Mr. Lennon. As you might guess, I did not receive any literary awards for that piece of writing. We did, however, receive several death threats and an offer to burn our house down.

 3. OUR GODLY LIFESTYLE

Third, we can expect persecution because of our lifestyle. Paul expressed it this way: "In fact, everyone who wants to live a godly life in Christ Jesus will be persecuted" (2 Timothy 3:12).

It is amazing to observe the wildly divergent reactions to the lifestyle of our Savior throughout His brief ministry. The ones who were open to His message of hope, salvation and healing fell down to worship at His feet. They wanted to be with Him and follow Him everywhere. But others—"religious types" in most cases—were repulsed by Him. Jesus threatened every aspect of their religious life. The mere mention of His name brought on feelings of anger and disgust.

The same will be true for us. Those who accept the Lord through observing our lives will be our very best friends. They will want to be with us and follow our example. But those who reject Christ will reject us, too. Our lifestyle will be considered "strange" and "offensive." This is the very essence of sharing in the sufferings of Christ.

RESPONDING TO PERSECUTION & PERPETRATORS

To this you were called, because Christ suffered for you, leaving you an example, that you should follow in his steps.

"He committed no sin,
    and no deceit was found in his mouth."

and the hint of a pugnacious character. She pursed her lips and wagged her head so that her hair swayed across her back. He wished he knew what was working under her skin.

"I'm going to visit Dana this weekend."

He sighed. "I'll miss you."

Her eyes bared her soul. "I'll miss you, too."

"I certainly hope your weekend doesn't completely unravel our relationship."

"How could it?"

"Dana's wicked tongue, that's how."

"If that's all it takes, then it wasn't much to begin with," she said, and he nodded reluctantly. "It'll give us some breathing room. Maybe I've been trying too hard. I'm tired." Wearily, she rolled her head around on her neck. "Trying to keep up with you is tough going."

"You shouldn't ever feel less than me. Don't let anyone imply that you don't write as well as I do. I certainly never said that. Never."

"You didn't have to come right out and tell me you're a better writer," she said, pretending to be engrossed in her manicure but gripped by the effort it took to reveal this small, petty part of her. "You got the job and I didn't. 'Nuff said." Tess pressed her lips together to keep them from trembling. Saying that aloud had been about as pleasant as being trampled by a rogue elephant. She wanted to know his reaction, but she couldn't look at him. Her courage deserted her, leaving her to stare at her fingernails as if they were the dearest things in the whole wide world.

"Tess, I hope you don't really believe that."

She started to laugh, but cut it off short when she heard the bitter edge. "Even back in college people recognized your superiority, didn't they? Do you think I'm so thickheaded I wouldn't get it by now? I don't have to try out for the team to know I'm too short to play basketball with the big boys."

He tread softly for he saw vulnerability in her features. Curving one hand at the back of her neck, he brought her head forward to rest on his shoulder. Her hair smelled of lilacs and her cheek was petal soft.

Anything other than the honest truth just wasn't good enough for this woman, he decided, and so he tipped her head back to look boldly into her eyes.

"The caliber of your writing had nothing whatsoever to do with your not getting my job."

Her smile was stopped short of fruition by a sudden frost. Her eyes turned to ice, and she inched away from him, breaking all contact.

"What do you mean? How do you know that?" Even her voice was chilly.

"I just know," he said, shrugging. "Remember when I ran into you in that hotel lobby? I was meeting Harry Caper. He told me about you vying for the job."

"Why didn't you tell me that before—like in Las Vegas when I 'confessed' to you?"

"I didn't want to hurt you. I felt awful . . . well, you can imagine."

She pushed him back and slid off the top of the washer. "Let's not leave anything to the imagination, Ames," she said, her tone like ice. "Let me put it this way—if your character was a movie, I'd give it a half-star rating!"

9

TESS STARTED TOWARD the door, bent on a Hollywood exit, although she knew she'd have to return soon for her laundry, when another thought caught up with her. It pinned her to the spot and spun her around to face Asher again, her glorious exit ruined.

"What do you mean, the caliber of my writing had nothing to do with my not being hired?"

Feeling like a man who had stepped into one bear trap with his free foot balanced over another, Asher stared at her, numbed by his ill-fated situation.

"Ames . . ." She strode toward him and waved her hand before his glazed eyes. "Is the doctor in?"

He pushed aside her hand. "I've had just about enough of your mean tongue."

"I asked you a question."

"And I'm not deaf, Maxwell." He glowered at her, but her glower had more right behind it, so he had to look away. He found himself staring at a sign proclaiming Not Responsible For Lost Or Damaged Goods. Oh, if only he could tack such a disclaimer on himself, he thought, because no matter what he did now he was going to damage Tess's goods, and she might just be lost to him forever.

"Well?" she goaded.

"Don't be in such a hurry," he said, almost growling at her for making him hurry to his and her destruction. "You're not going to like what I'm going to say."

"I'll be the judge of that," she said cheekily, crossing her arms and hitching her weight on one hip. "Let's hear it."

He leaned back against a washer, seeing the inevitability of his pitiful fate. "Okay, you asked for it. Maybe I should have told you before, but I thought it might . . . well, you know. . . ."

"Just tell me already!"

"Okay!" He cleared his throat, and his head bobbed as if each word were propelled from him. "I got the job because I'm a man."

She blinked once. Hard. "Run that past me again."

"Oh, it's so stupid." He wished the big boss was in front of him now so he could throttle the narrow-minded weasel for placing him in a no-win situation. "Harry Caper told me I was hired over you because Ben Albright is a bigot. Old Ben would rather deal with men, says they're easier to work with or some such rot. Harry Caper told me that's why I got the nod over you."

She didn't say anything for a minute, just stared at him, then her gaze wandered to that sign, and Asher wondered if her thoughts traveled the same byway as his. "I don't believe this. All this time I've felt inferior to you. And you let me go on thinking it."

"I wasn't sure if I should tell you. . . ."

"Wasn't sure?" Her gaze came snapping back to his, and derision misshaped her mouth. "Please, Asher, don't insult my intelligence. You didn't tell me because it was to your advantage not to."

"That's a dirty lie." Anger flashed through him, stood him up on his own two feet and made him face her. "I didn't tell you because I was afraid it would hurt you. And don't roll your eyes at me. That really infuriates me, Tess."

"You're not my superior anymore, so you can't tell me what to do."

He started to snap back at her, say something equally juvenile, but his good sense stopped him. Instead he took in a cleansing breath, and the rumbling anger inside him subsided. He laughed lightly, chidingly.

"This isn't funny, bud," Tess said, still fuming.

"Maybe not, *bud*," he retorted, "but you've got to admit, it's not high drama, either."

"I'm glad you can view it so objectively. Forgive me, if I can't." She pressed a fist between her breasts. "It hurts too much here to laugh." Swiping at tears in the corners of her eyes, she started to turn away. He reached out for her, and she batted his hand aside as if it were something disgusting. "Don't pity me and don't pacify me. I have every right to be furious, *so let me be furious*."

He backed off, hands held aloft in a show of submission. "Be my guest."

"I thought I'd just revealed something to you . . . something important . . . something I'd had trouble admitting to myself, much less to anyone else. It took so much out of me to tell you my darkest secret—that I'm not your equal." She shuddered as if it still hurt to say it aloud. "You've let me go on thinking you got the job because you were a better writer and a better reporter. You knew all along that talent had nothing to do with it, but you didn't tell me." The pain drained out of her, leaving only the hard glitter of resentment in her eyes. "All the time I was running to catch up . . . all the hours I sweated over finding the right phrase, the juiciest verb, the fatal metaphor, and for what? You tell me you got the job because you can grow a beard and I can't."

"Well, that's a more delicate way to put it than what I had in mind, but, yes. Exactly." Since his touch was unwelcome, he stuffed his useless hands into his pockets.

Tears welled in her eyes and her lower lip quivered. She hugged herself, warding off betrayal and futility. "That's just great. The next man I hear spouting off about how women have equal rights and we're all just whining to hear ourselves complain, I'm going to give him a double helping of knuckle sandwich." She popped one fist into her other palm to demonstrate. "I swear I will."

"I'll buy tickets to that," Asher said, extending her a smile. "In fact, I'll hold him while you hit him."

"I don't need you to do anything for me, Ames. Not ever again." Her brittle voice hurt more than any knuckle sandwich she could have thrown at him.

"Tess, you're not going to hold this against me, are you?"

"Why shouldn't I?"

"It's not my fault," he reasoned, but felt his patience separate. "I'm not the bigot."

"You kept the information from me."

"I thought it would hurt you more than help you."

"You had no right to make that decision for me."

"Okay, okay." He patted the air, anxious to end the discussion while he still held threads of his patience. "So I've told you now. Let's put it behind us."

Tess gathered her pain close, not willing to release it go yet. "I'm not letting you off the hook that easily."

"Me? I'm not the one who didn't hire you based on your gender."

"I know that, but you kept it to yourself, didn't you?"

"I told you—"

"I know what you told me, but it doesn't make it hurt any less."

"Tess, will you please try to see my point of view?" he pleaded, but her chilling silence forced him to accept her standoff. With a flick of his hand to show his aggravation, he started to leave, then thought better of it. He turned toward her again, and her cool regard brought his anger to the fore.

"You're right, Maxwell. You're absolutely right. I kept it from you. I'm small and mean and petty. I didn't tell you, because I delighted in knowing I only got the job because I have a wienie and you don't." He cackled, laughing into the role of the arch villain. "Does that make you feel better, Maxwell?" Then his ears caught up with his anger, and he shed the stupid act. "You know, our relationship *is* looking more and more like a bad situation comedy and less and less like the real thing. Maybe we should cancel us."

He let that hang for a moment, hoping she'd shake her head or show some kind of remorse, but she didn't. "Great," he muttered, feeling like a man who'd just shot himself in the foot. "We're canceled. You're free to insert someone else in my time slot, honey. Have a dandy time in Joplin with Dana the Downer. You two ought to have a ball hoisting me up by mine." Then he left before he made an even bigger fool of himself by begging her to forgive him for something he didn't even do.

"WANT TO GO SEE a movie?" Dana asked brightly.

"No." Tess groaned and settled more deeply into the easy chair. Packages and shopping bags circled her, evidence of an entire day in the mall. "I'm exhausted. Can't we just eat something and then prop up our aching feet and pass out?"

"You need to take more vitamins," Dana said. "I'll make a list of the best ones for you."

"Don't bother."

"Tess, you really should take better care of yourself."

"I'm fine. Just because shopping wears me out while it rejuvenates you doesn't mean I'm ready for a hospital bed." Tess leaned over the side of the chair and pulled a lemon-yellow blouse from one of the shopping bags. "This is going to look super with that suede skirt I've got at home."

"Mmm, maybe."

"What, maybe?" Tess challenged.

"Yellow isn't really your color, you know. Makes you look like a cadaver."

"Well, gee-whiz, thanks a pantsload." Tess dropped the blouse back into the bag.

"I didn't mean to hurt your feelings," Dana said. "I just thought you'd want to know."

"Yeah, especially after I've already bought the blouse." She tugged a pair of houndstooth-checked slacks from a flat box and ran her hand across the wool blend. Glancing up, she saw Dana's knitted brows and the fretful lines fanning from the corners of her dark eyes. "What now? Black and white are no-no's, too?"

"No, but that pattern makes you look hippy."

"What's with you?" Tess asked, losing all patience. "Ever since I arrived here, all you've done is run me down."

"That's not true!" Dana declared. She flipped her auburn hair back over her shoulders in a gesture of irritation.

"Isn't it?" Tess thought back to the first insult. "So far you haven't approved of my perfume, my hairstyle, the shade of my lipstick, my suitcase, my robe—"

"That thing is at least five years old," Dana cut in.

"So what?" Tess demanded. "It's comfortable. What else?" She took a moment to get back on track. "Oh, yes, this pair of jeans and my sweatshirt."

Dana wrinkled her nose in distaste as her gaze moved over Tess's Kansas City Royals sweatshirt. "Teenagers wear those things. Not grown women."

"Says you."

Dana shrugged. "If you want to dress beneath you...."

"I'm not as concerned with clothes as you. There are more important things in life than color charts and designer labels."

"Asher used to be concerned with how a person dressed. I guess he's lowered his standards."

The hatefulness behind that statement brought tears to Tess's eyes. She stared at the woman she'd counted as her best friend since she was nineteen and wondered if she'd been a fool all those years. Tess pushed up from the chair and grabbed the handles of the bags.

"I'm going to lie down for a while," she said, starting toward the guest bedroom.

"Tess, I didn't mean to demean you," Dana said, and Tess turned back to her.

Looking into Dana's brown eyes, Tess saw nothing remotely resembling sincerity. "Yes, you did, Dana. That's exactly what you meant to do."

"No, I'm only trying to—"

"Help me?" Tess asked, having heard that from Dana more times than she could tabulate. She shook her head. "No, I don't think so. But let me assure you of one thing—I'm onto your game. I understand now that you belittle people to make yourself seem superior."

"Tess, that's hateful! I never—"

"But it won't work with me anymore." She angled up her chin. "I know damned well I'm a knockout in yellow, no pattern in the world could make me look hippy, and Asher Ames thinks I'm the sexiest woman he's ever laid eyes on."

Leaving Dana with her mouth hanging open, Tess went into the guest bedroom and threw the shopping bags onto the bed. Hot tears slipped from her eyes. Asher's right, she thought. Dana wasn't an ally anymore, if she ever had been. She was merely a woman with an inferiority complex who could spot the same in others. But Tess was no longer frozen by her own lack of self-esteem, so her friendship with Dana was strained and on the brink of snapping in two.

Brushing aside her tears, Tess resigned herself to losing a close friend. Regardless of that loss, she felt like a winner.

AFTER PARKING THE CAR in a space in front of Asher's town house apartment, Tess switched on the interior lights for a quick check in the rearview mirror. She didn't look as if she had jet lag, but she felt it. Her weekend at Dana's had been anything but restful. Enlightening, yes; pleasant, no. As soon as the 747's wheels hit pay dirt, she had girded herself for a meeting with Asher. She meant to apologize and ask if they could try again. She wanted him in her life. She'd missed him. Where he had been there was now a dark, deep cavity.

She turned off the interior lights and left the security of the car, but she didn't go to the front door immediately. Instead she assessed the place he called home. Two-storied with a pitched roof, the sandy-colored brick town house probably rented for almost twice what her apartment did. Black ironwork enclosed a charming courtyard, complete with bird feeders and a birdbath.

Tess unlatched the heavy gate and pushed it open on hinges that barely squeaked. She made sure it was closed securely behind her before she approached the steps leading up to the door.

"When did you get back?"

The deep voice came from above, and Tess jumped back as if she'd been shot. She looked up almost fearfully, but no deity looked down from on high. It was just Asher, arms crossed on the balcony railing, face half-hidden by shadow.

"You scared ten years off me," she said. "This afternoon. I got back this afternoon. Can we talk?"

"Go ahead."

"On equal footing, please."

"As always."

"I meant, can I come in or will you come out?"

"The door's unlocked. I'm the orange one. Come on up."

Frowning at his clipped command, she ducked into the concealing shadows of his porch and found two doors, one orange and one green. Making sense of his directions, she let herself in. A flight of carpeted stairs confronted her. Halfway up, she could see the living room spread out to her left, lit only by a small lamp sitting atop an entertainment center. There was a minimum of furniture: a couch, rocking chair, coffee table, end table, floor lamp beside a recliner. A tabby cat lay on the back of the sofa, its bushy tail swishing cautiously, its eyes wide and staring.

The kitchen, Tess noted, was spic-and-span, while her whole apartment cried out for a wet mop and a bottle of pine cleaner. All in all, Asher was a better housekeeper than she, but then she could say the same about nearly everyone she knew.

The apartment's layout had fooled her. From the outside it looked to be a two-storey town house, but it wasn't. The apartment next to it, the one with the green door, took up the lower story, while Asher's occupied the level above. She adjusted her guess at the rent he paid and decided hers stacked up evenly.

Rounding a corner, she entered his bedroom. It was dark. Nature provided the only illumination. The sliding glass door was open. A breeze scampered in, billowing the sheer draperies. Gliding past the simple double bed, Tess let her fingertips skate across the black satin comforter. Black satin and a simple double bed, she noted, readjusting her assumptions of Asher Ames. No fancy lighting or spacious water bed. He continued to surprise her.

"Yoo-hoo," she called, and a bulky shape shifted on the balcony. She leaned across the threshold. Asher sat in a redwood chair, his legs outstretched, bare feet propped on the railing. "I didn't know you owned a cat," she said.

He motioned toward the other chair. "I don't."

"But there's one—"

"She's just visiting."

"Oh, an overnight guest." Tess raised her eyebrows, suggesting impropriety as she slid onto the chaise. "I guess I should have called first."

Asher cut his gaze her way and allowed himself to smile. "Did you come to make up?"

She pulled her legs up tight against her body. "I stopped by to calmly discuss our differences."

Asher chuckled. "You came to apologize."

Tess shook her head. "No, no. I had every right to be upset with you. You should have—" She sensed his frowning countenance and edited her speech. "*We* should have discussed how and why you got the job right at the beginning."

"I wanted to, but I didn't know if you'd want to know that I already knew."

"Speak English, please."

"Oh, hell, Tess." He shot up from the chair and sat beside her. Gripping the armrests, he successfully imprisoned her. "I missed you all damned weekend. We've acted like a couple of idiots."

"Is that so?" Tess looked around her knees and saw the sincerity etched on his face. She squirmed, laughed a little under her breath and eased her legs down so that she wasn't cramped any longer. "That's better," she said, then sucked in a breath when he nuzzled her neck.

"Much better. Tess..." He raised a hand to her shoulder and stroked from collarbone to wrist. She felt delicate and he sensed a trembling beneath her skin. Moonlight painted her face. Shadows pooled, then moved aside to let him see her more clearly. "You look tired. How was the trip?"

"Lonely. Just like your weekend."

"I'm glad." He traced a thin blue vein on the inside of her wrist with his fingertip. They were both more fragile than they were ready to admit, he thought. Especially with each other. "Sometimes I think we should have gone slower, taken more time—"

"You regret Las Vegas?"

"No." The word burst from him. "No, not at all. Not in the least." He tipped his head sideways and worry clouded his eyes. "Do you?"

"No, I guess not."

"But you're not sure?"

"Doesn't it seem as if it were a dream and now we're wide-awake?"

He smiled briefly. "Yes, sometimes, but no regrets. I wanted you, and what's happened between us is so rare." Asher lifted her small hand and kissed the back of it. "This whole thing about us competing for the same job was blown way out of proportion."

"Maybe I take it more personally than you do. After all, you got the job."

"And you're holding that against me?"

"No, but it would have helped my self-esteem if you'd told me before *why* you got the job. In fact, you should have told me that you knew I'd applied for it."

"Tess, Tess," he hushed her, bringing her hand to his lips again. "We're doing it again. We're fussing about something that's history. Our timing was off, but our intentions were noble." He shrugged and made a comical grimace. "Let's not keep whipping ourselves."

She ran her fingers under the ribbed collar of his blue T-shirt. "When you're right, you're oh so right." Leaning toward him, she touched her lips to his. "While I was in Joplin I entertained a lovely idea about suing Ben Albright on the grounds of sexual discrimination." She laughed at his stricken expression. "But Dana said I'd be frozen in court litigation for the next two or three years. Her ex-husband is an attorney. Dana says you have to have lots of patience and money to get anywhere in the American legal system. I, unfortunately, have lots of neither."

"Well, you'd be on the right side, that's for sure."

"Yes, but it's enough right now for me to know that I'm perceived to be on your level."

"Why would you have ever doubted it?"

"Oh, Ash." She pressed her forehead to his and closed her eyes, weary with her own stupid sense of inadequacy. "You might think I've got tons of moxie, but it's a front for the most part. I'm a paper lion. I don't know why or how or when I began to doubt myself . . . but it happened. Every setback reinforced it. Every disappointment validated it." She lowered her brows and made a stern face. "'You're just not good enough,' became my lament. And I always thought you were so incredibly talented. It seemed so *easy* for you, while I struggled with every word, agonized about commas and semicolons. To me, you were Woodward and Bernstein all rolled into one."

"I find this hard to believe."

She opened her eyes to stare into his. "I don't go around telling everybody about my foibles."

"I'm honored you're telling me."

"Do you have any?"

"Dozens."

"Name one."

"When I really want something, I freeze up. Can't move. Can't think. I stand by and let whatever—or whoever—it is slip through my fingers."

She felt the smile start in her heart and find its way to her lips. "Are we talking about me now?"

"You guessed it," he said. His hands spanned her back, heating her skin through her shirt. "In all things, Tess Maxwell, I've always seen you as my equal. Please, *please* believe that."

"I do."

I do. In her imagination she saw herself standing beside Asher before a minister. The image jolted her. She recoiled, and Asher regarded her with shocked confusion.

"What? What did I do?" he asked, spreading out his hands in a beseeching way.

"We're getting too serious."

"I want to be serious, and what's more, I want to be taken seriously." Moving swiftly so she wouldn't have time to struggle, he stood up and lifted her into his arms. He laughed at her cry of alarm and blew hot air against her neck, making her shriek playfully. "Let's make love in my bed. I want you to christen it."

"Asher, I didn't come here to...I just wanted to talk."

"Sure, Tess. Never crossed your mind that I might be in dire need of that sweet body of yours after a weekend of going without, did it?" He carried her inside and then let her slip down until she was on her feet again.

The heat of him, the passion of him, the way he touched her, the way his mouth swooped to hers, made her crazily impulsive. She hurried to undress him before he could undress her. Once the top of her head socked his jaw, and she heard his teeth click together, but she scrambled on, intent on her mission. Their hands tangled, bumped, pushed, pulled, tugged... ripped.... The sound rent the air and made them both freeze.

"Asher, you tore my shirt!" She showed him the place where her sleeve had separated from the shoulder seam.

"Sorry. Wait...wait, don't pull...aww, ugh." He fell, his feet swept out from under him when she tried to pull off his jeans and jockeys before he was completely free of them.

"Oops. Are you hurt?"

He rubbed his bare backside and looked up at her. She covered her mouth with one hand. Pale light outlined her body and made the silk covering her hips and breasts shimmer. Asher untangled himself from the jeans and briefs and rose to his knees so he could press his mouth to her soft belly. He seesawed the slip of satin and lace down over her hips, her thighs, her knees. She used his shoulders to steady herself as she lifted one foot and then the other. Then she removed her sheer bra.

Looking up into her face, Asher thought she resembled a wood nymph with her hair strewn across her shoulders like autumn leaves and her eyes as green as moss on a riverbank. Even her skin held a golden luster worthy of a vision.

"Lord, you are so beautiful."

"Stop it," she said, her cheeks becoming as pink as a new rose. "I'm cute, but I'm no raving beauty."

He saw there was no convincing her of what he saw in her, no way he could make her see through her imagined flaws to the perfect soul of her womanhood. She moved from the circle of his arms to the bed, grabbed one corner of the comforter and swept it off. It fluttered up and around her like a matador's cape, settling across her shoulders, draping itself around her hips. With a skip, a giggle and a half turn, she fell onto the bed. The comforter crawled across her, exposing a length of thigh, a hint of nipple, the seductive curve of her waist.

The filtered light made her skin glow, her eyes glisten. His body responded. His flesh reached out to her, his heart hurtled itself against his chest wall. Every part of him ached, strained, pulsated.

He made a dive for her just as she sat up to untangle the comforter from around her long, silky legs. Asher had only enough time to grunt in alarm before he slid across the satin sheets and rapped his forehead against the edge of the bedside table.

"Oww, damn it!"

"Asher!"

He flopped onto his back, one hand on his forehead and his eyes tightly shut against the pain.

"Oh, Ash. I didn't know . . . are you okay, love?"

"Love?" He opened his eyes. "Say that again and I'll be as good as new. Better than new."

"Love," she said, letting the *l* roll off her tongue like a cube of sugar, then she forced his hand away from his forehead and her lips sweetened the red spot underneath. "Poor, darling Asher. I didn't know you were going to tackle me or I wouldn't have moved an inch."

He grinned, liking this side of her, although his head pounded in unison with his jaw and backside. "Oh, well. I'll survive."

"You'll be black-and-blue tomorrow."

"So what? If anyone asks I'll tell them you're a wild woman in bed."

She giggled and kissed his bump again. "I like that. I've always wanted to be known as a femme fatale. Like Dana."

"Dana?" He shook his head. "Dana was never that. You've always had an overblown image of her."

"I have? You didn't think she was one sexy little number, huh?" she asked with heavy skepticism.

"Dana was—probably still is—a lady with a flair for the facade. She puts on a good front, but behind that attractive surface is a woman with a passel of self-doubts and imagined slights."

"Are we talking about the same Dana?"

"She always thought everyone was out to get her or was saying things behind her back," Asher said, lost in his memories. "Maybe she's changed. Back in college she had a nasty habit of running people down so she'd feel superior."

Tess brushed his hair with her fingers while she considered his view of Dana. But three in a bed was one too many, she decided and slid down against the slick sheets. Dana slipped from her thoughts.

"I never took you for a guy who slept on satin sheets."

"I like the feel of them," Asher said, not embarrassed in the least. "They feel like your skin."

She wrapped him in the black comforter and pulled it tightly around them. Then she pelted his face with lightning-quick kisses, making him laugh and know the soaring happiness he'd thought he'd lost with his youth.

"I want to make sure there's not one inch of your face I haven't kissed," she explained. She ran her thumbs under his jaw and kissed him there. "Scratchy, but nice. Men have such interesting skin. It's not like satin. It's more like suede."

Lethargy seeped into him. He felt like a fat cat, full of himself and satisfied with his lot in life. Asher rolled onto his back, closed his eyes and sent up a grateful sigh.

"Just being in bed with you is heaven," he said after a few moments of companionable silence.

"Not quite." She stretched onto her side right up against him and ran the fingers of one hand through the mat of black hair below his navel. "This is nice, but it's not quite heaven." She arched one brow. "And I'm not talking about that place in Vegas."

"I know." He brought her hand to his lips, then moved it down his body again. The back of it brushed against his arousal, and then her fingers caressed his hot swollen flesh. "I need you, Tess. Like stars need night."

His body was positively bold, Tess thought. For a white-collar worker, he had a blue-collar body with lean, hard legs, firm buttocks and a flat, muscled stomach. His rib cage arched up like a mountain ridge. She ran her hands over his handsome landscape, the rest of her body following after until she was lying on top of him. She liked the fit of her valleys and his ridges and vice versa. Two so totally different landscapes merging perfectly astounded her. Even the steady, powerful rise and fall of his chest amazed her. If their positions were reversed and he placed his weight on her, she wouldn't be able to breathe evenly. But he could do it. Easily. Like a bellows.

His hands roused her from her rapt admiration, moving like a warm tide over her hips and back. He gripped her head, lifted it off his shoulder and held it fast. His tongue moistened her lips and electrified the inside of her mouth. He moaned and his breath entered her and infused her with restlessness. She sat astride him, arching her back so that her breasts lifted proudly and her hair streamed over her shoulders. His hands held rough magic. Her nipples tightened to sensitive buds of flesh. The flames of passion licked her belly.

Rising up on her knees, she moved to take him inside. The joining of their bodies seared them both, and they melted into one. Desire consumed her with the speed of a brushfire and, replete, she crumpled onto Asher's heaving chest. He was damp and his skin was aromatic with the scent of sex, of maleness. His hands smoothed over her, pressing into her curves, kneading the taut muscles in her thighs and shoulders.

"I'm my best self with you," he whispered against her hair.

She smiled and nestled against his side. He turned to face her, draped his arms loosely around her, pushed out his lips for a reaching kiss that barely made contact with the tip of her nose.

"Why can't we always be like this?" she asked.

"Because we'd be arrested."

She tweaked his ear, then caressed it. "You know what I mean. We get along so well when we're alone, but then the rest of the world shows up and spoils it all."

"Give us time. We've only just begun. It's not so unusual for two stubborn, competitive souls to butt heads now and then."

"I know, but the problem is we get angry with each other. We take it personally when we shouldn't."

"So let's make a pledge that whatever happens at work isn't personal." He held up his right hand. "I swear not to use my work against you."

She looked at his waiting palm. "Is that possible? When I scoop the next story, won't I be working against you?"

"When *you* scoop the next story?" he repeated dubiously.

"See? We're competing again."

"Okay, so let's promise to take off the gloves after work. We'll do our best to stay out of each other's way—professionally."

She heaved a sigh, gave a shrug and pressed her palm against his. She laced her fingers in his, and he gripped her hand as tightly as she gripped his. "Okay. So pledged."

"Feel better?"

"Yes." She smiled and snuggled closer.

"Good, because you might not like what I've done."

She puckered her brow. "I already don't like the sound of that." Craning back, she examined his innocent expression. "What have you done now, Asher?"

"I feel silly telling you after the promise we just made."

"Tell me," she insisted, burning to know.

"I might have found you a new job." He smiled, but it was a forced parody that bordered on a grimace. "Working for me."

10

GATHERING THE COMFORTER around her again, Tess sat up in bed. "What do you mean, working for you?"

Asher flung an arm across his eyes, unable to stand her flinty-eyed glare. "What I did, I did because I want the best for you. You deserve it. You certainly deserve more than you're getting at your newspaper."

"What did you do, Asher?" Tess repeated, losing her tolerance while cautioning herself not to fly into a fury before he'd given her good reason. When he didn't respond instantly, she jiggled his arm.

"I talked to Harry about an idea I've been kicking around for a few weeks. I'd like to overhaul our entertainment section and I asked Harry to hire you for a newly created position of television editor. I'd be entertainment section editor, but I'd concentrate on live performances and films." He sucked in a quick breath and rattled on, not giving her an opportunity to interject anything. "You know TV inside out. It would be a great opportunity for you, and it would increase the newspaper's esteem. You'd have two pages daily and an entire TV book on Sundays."

He lifted his arm and peeked underneath it. Tess's mouth had fallen open in shock. She pulled the comforter more closely to her body—using it as a shield, no doubt, he thought.

"You submitted my name without even asking me?"

"It's been done before, you know. The ball is still in your court."

"Yes, but why didn't you ask me first?"

"I'm impulsive." He flung out his arms in an open, vulnerable gesture. "Give me fifty lashes, then give my idea serious thought, will you? Like I said, I've been tossing this idea around in my head and I had a meeting with Harry. The subject of improvements came up and out popped my suggestions before I could stop them. I figured you'd blow a gasket, but I know you'll cool off and realize I did what I did because I believe in you."

"Thanks." She smiled and it took a lot out of her. "I just wish. . . ."

"What?"

"Nothing. I don't want to fight now." Scrambling from the bed, she drew the comforter around her, picked up her panties and his T-shirt and headed for the bathroom. "While I'm in here, it would be great if you'd whip us up something to eat. I'm famished, aren't you?"

"What's that mean?" he asked, rising up on elbows. From the back she looked like a child playing bride with the comforter pulled up to make a hood and following her in a bulky train. The color, however, wasn't exactly bridal.

"Any old thing will be fine. When it comes to food, I'm not picky." The closing door halved the last word.

The lock snapping into place severed any further communication.

"She's suddenly gone deaf," Asher said, his upper lip lifting in a snarl. He swung his legs over the side of the bed, then stood and padded to the bureau. He stared intently in the mirror, wondering if the past few weeks had added more gray to his hair, but it hadn't. Nevertheless, the woman was depleting. He'd never known anyone before who could pull so many of his emotional strings. One moment he was deliriously happy and the next he was wallowing in guilt or kicking his own butt for putting in a good word for her.

He told himself he shouldn't have sprung it on her like that, then shook his head. No, he'd gotten into trouble before for keeping her in the dark. He sent a glare toward the bathroom, where the sounds of her shower could be heard. Damned if I do and damned if I don't, he thought with a pang of annoyance.

After pulling on underwear and gray sweatpants, he went into the kitchen to wash up and throw something together in the way of a late dinner. The visiting cat gave him only a passing glance, but when he opened a can of tuna, she came running and rubbed against his leg.

"Oh, sure," he grumbled. "Now that I've got food, you like me. You really are shameless." He dumped a spoonful of the flaked tuna into a saucer and set it in a corner, out of his path. The tabby crouched over the snack and sent up a rumbling purr interspersed with smacking sounds.

Using a box of casserole fixings, Asher followed the directions, adding only water and tuna. Within half an hour he poured the steaming concoction of noodles, tuna, peas and water chestnuts into a shallow bowl and set it on the table. A pitcher of iced tea followed, then a plate of sliced rye bread and another of oatmeal cream cookies, his current favorite.

After he finished setting the table for two, he stood back, approving of the hodgepodge menu. It met all his criteria; it was edible and wouldn't produce ptomaine poisoning.

Tess appeared right on schedule, wearing his red bathrobe. Her hair was damp around her face from the shower, and her skin was pink. She tucked herself into a chair and examined the main dish inquisitively.

"Tuna casserole?" she said, looking from it to him. "Are you going to join me or just watch?"

"You look good in my robe," he observed. "It's kind of big on you. I bet if we tried, we could both get inside it." He chuckled at her wary glance. "Help yourself to the food." He laughed again as she wrestled with the overly long sleeves, having to hold the sleeve back with one hand while she spooned casserole onto her plate with the other. "So, did the shower cool you off?" he ventured.

"It was refreshing."

"And?"

"And this casserole is really tasty," she said, closing her eyes as she chewed on in apparent ecstasy.

"Come on, Maxwell." He propped his elbows on the table and cradled his stubbly chin in his hands. "Let's talk turkey. Are you going to take the job if it's offered?"

"Probably not."

"I knew it." He wilted like a deflated balloon. "You're the most stubborn woman I've ever met. Just because it's *my* suggestion, you dismiss it out of hand. You're always cutting off your nose to spite your face." He knew he was gesturing wildly, but he couldn't help it. It was all her fault, a voice buzzed in his head. She brought out the fanatic in him. "Forget that this might be the best opportunity your career has seen in a decade. Forget that you'll have room to write and review and analyze to your heart's content. Forget that you'll double your readership. Forget all that. It's *my* idea, so it stinks."

She bobbed one shoulder and the robe slipped, exposing her other shoulder and part of her breast. A jerk and a tug set it right again. "I don't want you as my boss, Asher."

"I'd be the best boss you've ever had."

"Probably, but it wouldn't work out for us. I feel it in my bones."

"You wouldn't even know you had a boss. I'd leave the television coverage in your hands. I swear it."

"Thanks, but I can handle my own career." She glanced at the casserole dish. "Go on. Eat."

"I can't until this is settled."

"It is settled. I don't want to talk about business now, Asher! Please."

"No, you're going to listen to me because it's for your own good," he said, shaking a finger at her before he could stop himself.

She looked up, down, all around. "I could swear I heard my father just now."

"So I'm being paternal. I don't give a damn."

Her rapt attention to the food rankled, but he recognized it for what it was—a diversion. He ran the side of his forefinger above his lip thoughtfully and decided she wasn't as cool, calm and collected as she appeared.

"You've got a big chip on your shoulder, Tess Maxwell, and it's high time somebody knocked it off." He savored her eye contact. "For heaven's sake, don't stand on the shore this time, wrapped in a shroud of self-righteousness and hurt feelings, while your ship sails."

She lowered her brows, and he didn't know if that meant she was perplexed or pissed off.

"Come aboard this time," he said, keeping with his nautical theme. "Stand at the wheel with me. It'll be fun. A great adventure for both of us." He thought his speech was seaworthy, but when the corners of her mouth dipped he knew his ship was sunk. "Okay, Tess. Listen up. It's true confession time."

He paused to gather his thoughts before launching his next battalion. "My biggest regret is that I didn't confront you when you failed to show up for work on the college newspaper after I was named editor. I thought about it, but I played it cool. Since then I've wished I'd gone to you and told you how much I admired your work, how much I needed you and how much I looked forward to working with you." He massaged the back of his neck where the muscles were beginning to knot. Did she know how much this took out of him, this baring of the soul?

"My editorship was bittersweet because of you," he went on. "You spurned me and everything else turned sour. I'd dreamed of all those long hours spent in your company and how it would lead to something more." He grinned, recalling one particular phrase he'd run through his mind back then. "You know, from layouts to makeouts." He chanced a glance at her and was surprised to see that he finally had her undivided attention. Her crooked smile emboldened him.

"I won't let you get away this time without knowing how I feel." He swallowed with difficulty, his sentimental words choking him. "If you turn away...if you reject me again, then you do so knowing where I stand...how I feel."

She dropped her fork and slid her hand toward him. Her fingers closed around his, squeezing for a moment before relaxing. "You're sweet."

"No, no, no," he said, wincing. "Don't tell me I'm *sweet*." He laced the word with a saccharine loathing that made her giggle, and he was glad. The injection of levity made them both relax. "Tell me I'm not making a total fool of myself."

"You're not," she assured him, misty-eyed. "I'm glad you told me how you feel. I admit I was wrong to turn my back on the college newspaper just because things didn't go as I had planned. You weren't the only one on the injury list. Not being named editor was major rejection." She widened her eyes dramatically. "*Major* rejection. I wasn't sure I'd survive it. But I can't keep building on top of what happened years ago. That's a shoddy foundation." She looked at him through her damp lashes. "I know you want instant answers, but I need time to think."

He nodded, understanding her desire to go slow. "Okay. But one more thing. Ever since college you were never far from my heart, Tess. Never far from my thoughts."

"And you were never far from mine, although I tried to deny it." She ran a finger along his jaw. "This bruise is already violet, and that bump on your forehead will be a shiner by tomorrow." She laughed under her breath. "You're going to look like a mugger's victim."

"You're not hopping mad at me?"

"No." She squeezed his hand. "Asher Ames, you are a hard man to stay mad at."

"I know." He fashioned a loony grin, and she laughed. The casserole tempted him now that he'd emptied himself of feelings stored too long. He dug the serving spoon into the tuna and noodles and awarded himself a generous portion.

"You're going to eat *now*?" she asked.

"I thought I would."

"Asher?"

"Hmm?"

"Asher?"

He tore his gaze from his plate. His robe was still in the chair across from him, but Tess wasn't. His gaze bounced automatically toward the bedroom. She stood in the doorway. Honeyed light fingered the curve of her spine and then gilded her backside as she disappeared from his view. Asher realized he was gripping the edge of the table, and his breathing had become little more than a rasp.

Finding his feet, he felt weak with a seizure of desire. As if led by an invisible chain, he followed in her footsteps. Only the rattle of dishes behind him broke the lead long enough for him to glance over his shoulder to see the cat going after what he'd left on his plate.

He took half a step toward the interloping cat, then he dismissed her for want of bigger game. "*Bon appétit*, old girl."

THRICE-DIVORCED Howard Bakjamin hovered near Tess's desk like a bee after a blossom.

He must have taken a shower in that after-shave, Tess thought, surreptitiously studying his odd behavior. He hardly ever ventured to her part of the vast newsroom, but all afternoon he'd never been more than a few feet away. Unable to stand his scrutiny another moment, Tess shoved aside her work and faced him.

"Can I do something for you, Howard? Something within reason, of course."

Those in earshot chuckled at her stipulation. Even Howard smirked, but then he smirked at nearly everything.

"I was just admiring the view, doll." He afforded her one of his self-described lady-killer smiles. "You're looking good today, baby. Mighty good. That gold blouse and black skirt is doing damage to my blood pressure."

"Thanks, Howie, baby." She gave a half laugh, finding his sudden attention comical. "So glad you approve of my wardrobe."

"I don't know . . . there's a glow about you," Howard persisted, deaf to her sarcasm.

"A glow, huh? Like sweat?"

"A womanly glow," he said, propping his hands on the edge of her desk to sway closer, further invading her space. His after-shave enclosed her in a sickly sweet cloud. It was all she could do not to gag. "I think you're the best looking gal on the staff."

Tess sat back in the chair and tapped her pencil against the desk blotter while she studied him. He stood straight again and hooked his thumbs in his belt, striking his cock-of-the-walk pose that never failed to tickle Tess. She barely managed not to laugh in his face.

"I think I'll buy you dinner tonight," he said, lowering his voice to an intimate whisper. "How does that strike you, doll?"

"Howard, did you happen to have lunch at the Press Club today?" she asked, beginning to understand why he found her so utterly irresistible.

"Yeah, I did. Were you there, too?" He slicked his thinning blond hair over the bald spot at his crown.

She shook her head. "I bet Asher Ames was there, wasn't he?" Just like Asher to read Howard perfectly, she thought, and to send him on a fool's errand. When Asher told her he would claim she was a wild woman if anyone got too nosy about his bruises, she never thought he'd actually do it!

"Yeah . . . I think I saw him there." Howard regarded her from the corner of his eyes, losing some of his self-assurance.

"Oh, it's nothing really." Sensing he was hooked, she tested the line. "Asher and I were talking last night and your name came up. He said you'd believe anything anybody told you." Tess noted Howard's deepening color. "Even if he told you some fool story about—" She flung up a careless hand. "Oh, I don't know, about me being a sex-starved Amazon. Even if he told you a story like that, he said you'd buy it hook, line and sinker. But I defended you, Howie. I told Asher he was all wrong about you." She hoped to mire him in her syrupy smile.

He chuckled and started backing away, trying to fight his way out of the quicksand. "Right . . . well, that's good of you. Ames has got a big mouth. You ought to keep better company. Anyway, I'd better get back to work. They don't pay me to flap my jaws."

"About that dinner . . ." she said, letting it hang in the air between them like a taut string before snipping it, "I can't."

"No problem. Really."

Tess smiled at his back. Howard made fast tracks to his desk and hid behind his stack of paper. Tess laughed silently at Asher's mean joke. She opened her briefcase and took out the mail she'd picked up from her post office box that morning. Flipping through it, she recognized a bill and a political flier. The next three envelopes made her heart climb into her throat and her palms grow damp. She glanced around nervously, feeling like a traitor because she held in her hands responses to her job inquiries. She opened them quickly, scanning the letters inside and telling herself she was dreaming. All three—two newspapers and one syndication service— were favorable. The newspaper editors wanted to set up meetings with her. The director of the syndicate actually made a job offer.

Tess closed her eyes and rubbed them vigorously. She read the letters again, then pressed the heel of her hand hard against her mouth to keep from giving a joyous whoop.

She'd sent her résumé and newspaper clippings with only half a hope of actually receiving any nibbles. Dana had reinforced her doubts by cautioning her not to get her hopes up, pointing out that the positions were probably already filled. But all three had bitten.

Maybe I'm better than I thought, she mused, then realized how unsure of herself she sounded. *Of course, I'm good. Better than good.* Giving a nod, she approved of her sturdy self-image.

She read the letter from the syndicate again and liked the job description. She could use Kansas City as her home base, and she'd be given travel expenses plus a generous salary while covering both the television and film industry. Tess folded the letters carefully and returned them to their envelopes. She tucked them into an inside pocket of her briefcase, added a couple of files, then closed the lid. Her hands were shaking. Pride spread within her like a new dawning.

Tonight she'd decide how to answer the inquiries, but she was already leaning toward accepting the syndicate's offer. In many ways, it was the job she'd dreamed of ever since college.

She gathered the rest of her belongings and left the office and the building. Half an hour later she entered her apartment, threw her briefcase and purse onto the couch and went directly into the bedroom. Bursting with the good news, she dialed Asher, but Skip said he would be out of the office for the rest of the afternoon. She tried his home, but there was no answer. After striking out twice, she went for strike three and phoned Dana. While the phone rang she kicked off her shoes and sat on the side of the bed and prayed Dana would be home. She *had* to tell someone or she'd fly into pieces!

"Hello?"

"Dana!"

"Hi, Tess."

"Guess what?"

"You know how I hate conversations that begin with 'guess what?' Tess. If you've got something to tell me, just tell me."

Tess smothered a giggle. "I got three job offers in the mail today. Three! Well, only one of them is a firm offer. The other two want to set up interviews. Isn't that great?"

Several seconds ticked by before Dana responded. "Sure. Are the offers any good?"

"Well . . . of course." Tess sputtered a moment, her enthusiasm diluted by Dana's less than thrilled tone. "They're great offers. One of them is from a syndicate—"

"You wouldn't want that."

"Why not?"

"A syndicate? I thought you liked working for a newspaper."

"I do, but if I work for a syndicate my pieces would run in lots of newspapers instead of just one." Tess gritted her teeth, irritated that the conversation wasn't going as she'd expected it would. She plucked a tissue from a dispenser and dabbed at the perspiration beading on her forehead. Glancing at the thermostat in the hallway, she willed the air conditioner to kick on. "Dana, is something wrong? I mean, did I phone at a bad time?"

"No, I just got home from bridge club."

"You're the first one I've told," Tess said, trying to make Dana see the importance of her news. "I'm really excited about the syndicate offer. I can stay here in Kansas City."

"And we all know why you're so *wedded* to that place, don't we?"

Tess frowned at Dana's surly tone. "Because it's my home."

"Because it's Asher Ames's home, you mean."

"I didn't want to leave Kansas City before Asher moved here. But, I admit, leaving him would be hard now."

"Can you take some sound advice?"

"Dana, please don't trash Asher. I know you don't—"

"Okay, if you aren't willing to hear a reasonable voice, fine," Dana interrupted, clearly offended.

"All right, what's the advice?"

"I don't know why I should bother. Your very tone tells me you have no intention of even considering what I have to say."

"Say it, Dana. I'm listening."

"I'm telling you this because we've been friends for ages. I know you. I know you better than you know yourself. Better than Asher Ames knows you, that's for sure."

"Dana, out with it already," Tess pleaded.

"I think it would be good if you leave Kansas City. If you leave now, you leave with your dignity intact."

"Meaning?"

"Meaning you can hold your head up. Nobody can say you were dumped."

"Dumped by Asher, you mean." Tess gathered handfuls of the bedspread as her aggravation mounted. She told herself to keep cool, not to let Dana get to her, but it was difficult. When it came to Asher, Dana was merciless, running him down at every turn and constantly warning Tess that she was in for a big fall. The air conditioner roared to life, and Tess fell back onto the bed in relief.

"He has a short attention span," Dana said. "It's not about you, it's about him. I know you think you're the only woman for him—"

"I never said that," Tess cut in. "And whatever happens, I'll survive. So don't worry about that, Dana. I can handle whatever Asher dishes out. Besides, I didn't call to talk about him. I just wanted to tell you my good news. At least, *I* think it's good news."

"So do I. Since you don't have a family, I know how important your career is to you and—"

"I have a family, Dana. I didn't crawl out from under a rock," Tess cut in.

"You know what I mean. I just have a feeling you might be happier away from Asher, and I can't see you working for anything other than a metropolitan newspaper. But, you do what you think is best."

Tess sighed into the phone receiver, wanting Dana to hear her aggravation. "I'll let you go. Call me sometime."

"I will."

"'Bye."

"Always good to hear from you."

Tess replaced the receiver and wished she hadn't made the call. Dana had single-handedly ruined a perfectly wonderful mood. As she removed her work clothes and changed into baggy jeans and a camp shirt,

Tess tried to regain her equilibrium. She had a right to be happy, she told herself, and Dana was wrong to dampen her good news with dire predictions of impending heartbreak. It seemed that's all Dana talked about anymore. Just one reason after another why Tess should quit seeing Asher before he took a powder on her.

"She's so *positive* he's going to break it off with me," Tess muttered darkly as she went into the living room. "I swear, Dana, sometimes I wonder whose side you're on."

The message light was blinking on her answering machine so she pressed the play button. Asher's voice commanded the room.

"Hello. You're not home yet, so I'll call back later. I thought we might eat dinner together or something if you don't have a lot of work you have to do or something. Why is it I sound like a blithering idiot when I have to leave messages on these things?"

Tess smiled and dropped to the couch to wait for the next message.

"It's me again. Cancel that dinner offer. Something came up, but I'm not telling you anything about it because you're too good. If I let one little thing slip, you'll be on it like a duck on a beetle and scoop me, you little devil you." His warm laughter made Tess join in. "Last night was great, wasn't it?" His low voice made her throb inside. "We're going to be okay, aren't we? I hope so. I feel good about us, don't you?"

Tess switched off the machine. She gave a minute's thought to making some calls to find out who or what Asher might be covering that evening, but she decided to order a pizza and watch a favorite movie on the VCR instead. Tonight she'd indulge herself and tomorrow she'd slay the dragons.

She reached for the phone to dial the pizza delivery number. Let Asher have his scoop. It wouldn't take her long to even the score again, she thought, smiling at her new self-assurance.

11

SITTING NEAR THE FRONT of the darkened theater, Tess jotted down a few key words to remind her of her reaction to the filmed car chase that had just ended in a scream of tires and crumpled metal. She turned to a new sheet in her notebook and adjusted the angle of the battery-powered minilight to better illuminate the page.

She winced at the final spate of supposedly humorous dialogue passing between the actor and actress, then sighed regretfully when a few people around her actually laughed at the inane patter. She wondered if Asher was among those guffawing. She ached to know, but resisted the urge to turn around and try to spot him. The theater was full for the free sneak preview, so finding Asher would be nearly impossible. They'd arranged to meet at the theater, but Tess had insisted on sitting apart, afraid his reaction to the film would color her own or distract her.

He'd agreed and had sent her ahead of him while he chose a seat at the rear of the theater. The action-drama was cut from the antihero mold and so predictable Tess had the feeling she'd seen it before, many times before. She'd even managed to mouth some of the dialogue along with the characters, getting only a word or two wrong.

Credits began to roll, and Tess made a few more notes before switching off the book light and tucking the notebook into her purse. When she looked up again, Asher was waiting for her at the end of the aisle. Looking debonair in his double-breasted suit, he offered his arm as she approached.

"If you're nice to me, I'll buy you an ice-cream cone."

"How did you know that's what I was craving?"

"You're a woman of simple tastes," he answered.

"Why do you think I'm dating you?"

"Ha-ha," he said without cracking a grin. "Great flick, huh?"

"Ha-ha."

He broke stride. "You *did* enjoy it, didn't you?"

"Did you?"

"Yes, I thought it served its purpose."

"It did, if its purpose is to appeal to the brain dead." She swept ahead of him out the door and onto a bricked square in front of the theater. A multitiered fountain dominated the area. Marble lions roared water, and each was ridden by cherub-faced boys holding aloft shallow bowls from which streams dribbled over the sides. Sprays shot up into the air, each at a different height and colored a different hue from deep purple to pale blue.

Asher ducked into the ice-cream shop next door and emerged a few minutes later carrying two butterscotch pecan double-dippers on sugar cones. He handed one to her along with a napkin.

"Didn't you think the film was exciting?" he asked between licks. "I thought that scene in the prison camp was chilling."

"Chilling, yes. It left me cold."

He shook his head disapprovingly. "You're reacting like a woman instead of a reviewer."

"I value my woman's intuition. When my femininity shrinks from something, I pay attention to it. If men had the same intuition, we wouldn't be seeing films that glorify brutality and barbarians." She walked toward the fountain, drawn by the romance of it. "Are you going to file your story tonight?"

He glanced at his watch and cursed softly. "I wanted to, but it's already eleven so I won't be able to make the midnight deadline." He bowed at the waist. "You may have this one first, madam."

"How kind of you, sir." She sat on the low wall, her back to the dancing waters, and patted the concrete next to her. "Care to join me?"

"Don't mind if I do." He sat next to her and held one of her hands, his fingers lacing through hers in a comfortable reflex.

"We could be in a movie," Tess said. "A fountain for a backdrop and two lovers holding hands and eating ice-cream cones. Right out of a musical, don't you think?"

"Or a Norman Rockwell painting."

"No," she said, scrutinizing him. "You're not inno-cent-looking enough for that."

"Oh-ho, and *you* are?" he challenged with a laugh. "Where's your halo? Did you leave it at home to-night?"

She nudged him with her elbow and devoted herself to the rest of her ice-cream cone, ignoring him only outwardly. Still holding her hand, he brought it to rest atop his thigh, and that simple gesture took on an in-timacy she knew was completely out of proportion to the act. She remembered his message left on her an-swering machine.

"What you said last night about feeling good about us," she ventured.

He nodded. "I do, don't you?"

"Yes, but I wasn't sure how you felt before. We've had our ups and downs."

"Who hasn't?"

"Sometimes it feels like we don't agree on very much at all."

"We agree on important things." He looked up at the starry sky. "We agree that nights like this are gifts, that slow, deep kisses are an art form, that butterscotch pe-can ice cream is one of man's greatest achievements and that silk sheets make for great sex."

She smiled. "That's true. We certainly agree on the key issues of our time."

"You haven't said a word about my article this morning about the new regional theater director."

"That's what you stood me up for last night?"

He shrugged. "Duty called. You know how it is."

"Who tipped you to the story?"

"Skip's girlfriend's mother is on the theater's board of directors."

Tess made a derisive sound. "I never thought of Skip Bailey as a valuable news source. Oh, well, he *should* be good for something."

Asher growled like a cat. "Nasty, nasty." He released a sharp laugh. "Skip is short on experience, but he's getting there."

"It's a shame the newspaper couldn't hire you an experienced reporter instead of making you play nursemaid to a college kid. Lucky for Skip he's got a top-notch teacher."

"When are you going to give your two weeks' notice and join the zoo?"

"I haven't even been offered the job," she reminded him.

"You will be by the end of the week. Harry's been given the go-ahead."

"You're telling me that Good Old Boy Ben has decided to hire a woman for an editor's position?"

He nodded. "Guess we won him over."

"You did. I've only met the old geezer once in my whole life. Once was enough, believe me."

A cloud appeared on his horizon. "You're not going to refuse this offer just because Ben Albright is a narrow-minded fool, are you?"

"No."

"Good." He covered his heart with his hand in a show of relief. "You had me worried there for a second."

Tess twisted around to watch the fountain's show. "I talked to Dana yesterday and it really upset me."

"Why?"

"Because you've opened my eyes to something about her I couldn't see before." She laughed, but it was a nervous release. "I don't know whether to thank you or kick you."

"I know which one *I'd* prefer." He touched her cheek tentatively. "So what did Dana say that upset you?"

"You can imagine how thrilled she is that I'm seeing you."

"What business is it of hers?"

"She's my friend. She cares about me." Tess looked down at their clasped hands. "Or so I've always thought."

"Now you're not sure?"

"You told me that Dana had a habit of running people down to make herself look good." She lifted her gaze to his. He nodded, silently telling her he understood. "When you said that, it started me thinking. I don't know, maybe I'm overly sensitive lately, but when I told her about the job she wasn't excited for me. Not at all."

"You told her you'd be working with me? Notice I said 'with' and not 'for' because that's how I see it, Tess. I won't be your boss. I don't want us to have that kind of relationship."

"Ash, I've had a few other offers besides yours."

He sat back in stunned silence for a few moments. "Since when?"

"Yesterday I heard from three interested parties." She squeezed his hand, trying to share the excitement. "It bowled me over, but when I told Dana she acted as if it were nothing. It made me think about what you'd said and about all the times I turned to Dana for support, but she never really looked out for me. I don't know why I didn't see it before. Like when I didn't show up for work on the newspaper in college...."

"What about it?"

"Well, I told Dana about how hurt I was not getting the editorship and how it would be hard to swallow my pride and work for you."

"And Dana told you not to work with me, right?"

"That's right."

"Sounds like something she'd do. Back in college, when you didn't come to work, I went to your apartment. You weren't there, but Dana was. I told her I'd come to ask you to be my assistant editor, but she told me you'd never—I repeat, *never*—work on my staff. She said you thought I was incompetent."

"She what?" Tess asked, shocked.

"That's what she said, and like a damned idiot, I believed her. She knew it would drive a stake through my heart. She always knew how to make me retreat."

"She's doing it again, trying to keep us apart. She even went so far as to suggest that I leave Kansas City."

Asher's laugh was acidic. "This town ain't big enough for both of us? It's funny. Dana doesn't want me, but she doesn't want anyone else to have me, either."

"Don't be so sure she doesn't want you," Tess cautioned. "Have I been blind all these years? When I look back I keep remembering times when I needed encouragement, and Dana never came through. She always took the low road. I guess I thought she was preparing me for the worst, but maybe she expected the worst all along."

"Or hoped for it."

"She's my friend."

"And what am I, chopped liver?"

She stared at him, shocked into silence by his biting tone and the angry expression marring his face. He pulled his hand from hers and faced front.

"You told Dana, but not me about your job offers."

"I tried to call you last night."

"What about this morning?"

"I knew I'd see you tonight. What's your point?"

"I'm jealous—again. This isn't the first time I've felt that Dana was standing between us." He stood up and shoved his hands into his pockets. "Let's go."

"You're overreacting, Asher." She got to her feet and clutched his jacket sleeves, giving a little tug to get past his indignation. "Telling Dana was second nature, and I was going to talk to you about it last night but you were busy working, so I'm trying to tell you now. Are you going to listen or punish me for messing up my order of importance? Come on," she urged, shaking him again. "Give me a break, will you?"

"It just infuriates me that you let Dana manipulate you, try to run your life even when she doesn't have your best interests at heart." He shook her off and stepped away from her, even turning his back.

Anger rose up, fast and furious. "You want Dana to butt out."

"Right."

"So *you* can manipulate me."

"What?" he asked, half-turning toward her.

"You're the one who submitted my name for a job without telling me about it first, aren't you? And now you're mad because I've submitted my résumé to other places. Excuse me, Mr. Ames!"

His laughter singed. "I don't need this aggravation. You do what you want. I'm going home to peace and quiet."

"Go!" She glared at him as he strode off toward the parking area, then whirled around to face the fountain. The water blurred as tears filled her eyes. She had so much to tell him, she thought miserably, as her anger subsided and the hurt set in. She'd wanted to tell him about the job offers and why her decision to accept one of them would be perfect, not just for her but for her *and* him. She'd wanted to tell him that he'd been the one who'd made her believe in herself enough to reach out for better things.

Spinning around, she saw his car zip from the lot and along the street. Fury seized her again, and she wiped the tears from her eyes and ran toward her car. Damn him, he wasn't going to walk out on her just when she'd decided to spend the rest of her life with him.

Once inside her car, she touched up her makeup, thinking she'd cried more in the past few weeks than she had in years.

"Love is such a picnic," she drawled to herself in the rearview mirror.

She didn't realize to what extent she'd broken the speed limit until she pulled into the parking lot of Asher's complex and saw him getting out of his car. When he recognized her, he did a double take.

"I didn't know your car had a supersonic gear," he said as she slammed the door and strode toward him. "If ever I saw a woman on the warpath, you're her."

"I refuse to allow you to sulk all night when we should be engaged in an adult confrontation."

Gripping her upper arms, he yanked her to him, and his mouth stung hers. "I don't sulk," he said against her lips. "I simmer."

She gave herself over to the mastery of his next kiss, then the seductive laziness of the next one.

"Do you have any idea of how sexy you look when you're fighting mad?" he whispered. He palmed her backside. "Or maybe it's got something to do with parking lots. When you're in one, I can't keep my hands off you."

"Or maybe friction gets us hot," she said, realizing how quickly anger changed to desire. Pushing him away with a husky laugh, she recalled that other parking lot and the eavesdropping attendant. She glanced around and was glad for their solitude.

"Let's go inside and thrash this out," she suggested. "I know we both have to go to work tomorrow—me at the crack of dawn and you a few hours later—but I won't be able to sleep at all with an ax hanging over my head."

"An ax?" he repeated with a dramatic flair.

"Yes. That's how I feel when you go off in a huff and leave me to worry about me and you—about us."

"Okay," he said, curving an arm at her back. "Come inside. But I have a right to be ticked off."

"What right?"

"A lover's right, damn it all. Whatever I've done, I've done to help you."

"What am I, your ward?" she shot back, then climbed the stairs ahead of him.

"Forgive me for wanting only the best for you. Lord, you have a great rear, Maxie. I swear, it's heart shaped."

At the top of the stairs, she turned to confront his rakish grin. "Let's keep my derriere out of this for the moment, okay?"

"Okay." The grin fell away. He went to the couch and dropped there. "You're not coming to work with me, are you?"

His disappointment tore at her heart. She perched on the edge of the lumpy couch and refused to take the easy way out by simply making love to him. Some problems transcended that, and this was one of them.

"I should have told you about it before I put your name up for consideration," he said, resting his head against the back of the couch. "But that's not any reason for you not to consider the job."

"I have considered it."

"Sure you have," he said, his tone calling her a liar.

"I have, Asher," she said again, this time more firmly. "I've considered all my options."

"You don't get it. I wanted you to take the job and stay put. Here with me." He shrugged. "So there you have it. My reasons weren't completely altruistic."

She laid a hand on his chest. "I *am* staying put. I'm going to work for Falstaff Syndicates."

He raised his head to look at her. "Falstaff? You got an offer from Falstaff?"

She nodded, pleased he was impressed. "That's right."

"Doing what?"

"Covering television *and* film. And I can stay in Kansas City. Increase in pay and travel expenses included," she added. "Plus a great insurance and retirement program."

"Falstaff is known for looking after its people." He rose from the couch and paced aimlessly, pausing to inspect a brown leaf on a plant and pitch an old newspaper into the trash. "Congratulations, Maxie. Sounds like a great job."

"Sounds like you're less than thrilled."

"I'm trying to be big about this, so give me some credit."

"You and Dana should team up. You two really know how to bring somebody down." She adjusted the shoulder strap of her purse and stood up. "Maybe it would be better if we talk about this tomorrow."

"No, let's talk about it now. You're right." He held his arms out from his sides. "I'm a tranquilizer. But I've been thinking about how great it will be when we're working together." He laughed at himself. "Going to work together every morning, having lunch together, coming home to make love every afternoon and evening." His gaze unsettled her; it was so direct, so naked. "You're my obsession, Tess. When it comes to real devotion, absolute faith in a person—" He shrugged helplessly. "I'm a neophyte, so you'll have to forgive some of my trespasses and my ugly moods." He released a long breath. "At least you're not moving to the far reaches of the universe."

"You never let on before that you cared where I lived. When I told you about looking for other work you didn't say one word!"

"I know, but my heart broke in half." He stared at the ceiling and blinked away the glimmer of tears. "I wasn't ready at the time to let you know about my Tess-obsession. Besides, I figured I'd solve that problem by hiring you."

"Asher, your dreams of us working together in perfect harmony are just that—dreams."

"Well, that's obvious now that you've decided to take another job."

"Apart from that, you're still dreaming. Our working harmoniously side by side is about as realistic as our writing the same review about the same film. Face it. Professionally, we butt heads, and working for the same newspaper wouldn't magically alter that."

"We've been butting heads because we work for competing newspapers."

"It goes beyond that."

"I don't think so."

"Asher, I like competing with you."

His eyes widened. "You do?"

"Yes. Don't you like it just a little?" She closed one eye in a seductive wink. "Gets your blood boiling, doesn't it? Makes you hot to trot. Heats up your griddle. Fires your rotisserie. Broils your potatoes. Braises your—"

He put a hand over her mouth. "Stop already! I get the picture." Withdrawing his hand, he replaced it with his mouth. His lips stroked hers, then moved back and forth. He caught her hands and brought them around him. "Speaking of starting fires, I think we can do it if we rub up against each other a few more times."

"Starting fires has never been a problem for us. Controlling them is where we need work." She dodged his lips. "I take it you're all better now? You understand why I'm not going to work for you?"

"Because you're stubborn?"

"No." She pushed him back. "The problem, as I see it, is that we've been getting in each other's way because we've been hemmed up in the same corral. By putting myself in a different one, we can compete without stomping all over each other. But I think your idea of beefing up the entertainment section is great."

"As long as you're not part of it."

"You're purposely making this difficult, aren't you?"

"No, I'm just not entirely ready to see everything your way."

"Asher, I need something I don't have to share with you." Grabbing his lapels, she put a pleading note into her voice. "Come on, big guy, be happy for me."

"Does it mean that much to you that I be overjoyed?"

"Yes, damn it! It means everything to me." The lightness in her tone subsided. "*You* mean everything to me. Don't you know that by now?"

He covered her hands and brought them to his lips for a kiss. "Glad to hear it. If you're happy, I'm happy."

"No, that won't cut it. I want you to understand that this is right for both of us. We won't be competing for the very same audience, and that will take the stress off our relationship," she explained. "Believe it or not, I considered what would be best for us. Was I wrong to do that? I wasn't taking anything for granted, was I?"

"Doubting Thomasina," he chided. "Didn't I just tell you I was obsessed? What more do you want, woman?"

"Obsessed isn't exactly the word I wanted to hear," she admitted. "But I guess it'll do in a pinch."

"Lucky for you, I'm a man of many words." He drew aside her shirt collar and dropped a kiss at the base of her neck. "Lust?"

"That's a good one."

His lips traced a vein up her neck. "Satyriasis?"

She laughed, then sucked in her breath when his teeth nipped her earlobe. "Mmm, I remember that one."

"Libido?"

"That's a nice one."

His mouth plucked at hers. "Love."

"Ahh," she breathed. "*That's* the one I was waiting for. Do you love me, Asher?"

"Only as much as you love me."

"Then you're saturated with it." She hopped into his arms and buried her face in the side of his neck as he carried her into his bedroom. "I'm so glad I came after you tonight. I have a feeling you're going to make me very, very glad of it."

"Before the night is over we're going to be downright delirious, sugar," he promised, sitting on the bed with her.

"Asher, will you marry me?"

He showed only an instant of surprise, then his brows formed a deep vee. "You're always scooping me, aren't you?"

"Will you marry me?" she asked, popping the buttons out of their slips to expose his chest to her stroking hands, her wet tongue.

"No, because *you're* going to marry *me*."

"Asher, let's marry each other," she revised.

"You mean, share the byline?"

"Yes. I like that." She kissed his smiling mouth. "I like that a lot." Then she drew away. "You do understand why I'm not going to work with you, right? Why I need something all my own?"

He nodded. "I think it's best that you have a job that doesn't have my fingerprints all over it."

"I like that, too. You do have a way with words." She placed his hands on her breasts and raised one brow in a come-hither gesture. "We'll get along just fine if you keep your fingerprints off my career, but all over my body. Agreed?"

"We are, where that's concerned, in total agreement," he assured her, pushing her blouse off her shoulders and running his hands over her smooth skin. "We might disagree on movies and TV shows and every other kind of entertainment, but when it comes to loving each other—" He kissed the hollow of her throat, her chin, her eyelids, her parted lips. "Tess, honey, we're an epic!"

She laughed and flung her arms around his neck. "A four-star, thumbs-up smash hit," she confirmed, then gave him her own personal seal of approval.

COMING NEXT MONTH

#293 THE ADENTURER Jayne Ann Krentz (Ladies and Legends, Book 2)

When romance writer Sarah Fleetwood hired ex-adventurer Gideon Trace to help her locate an old family heirloom, she got more than she bargained for. Gideon was the image of the hero she'd depicted in so many of her books—mysterious, dangerously appealing...but unavailable. Sarah had to figure out what made him tick—or forego the happy ending....

#294 ONLY HUMAN Kelly Street

Librarian Caitlin Stewart was just getting over her painful past when Lee Michaels charged through her carefully placed blocks. His investigation into football recruitment violations pointed to Caitlin's late husband. Lee would need all the right moves for the most important play of his life—getting Caitlin to love him.

#295 RIPE FOR THE PICKING Mary Tate Engels

When wounded law-enforcement officer Brett Meyer returned to his father's New Mexico ranch, he received a hero's welcome—from everyone except Annie Clayton. Annie found his presence unsettling. Her life was firmly rooted in her struggling apple farm and Brett was restless to move on. Annie feared he'd leave again...and take her heart with him.

#296 GUARDED MOMENTS JoAnn Ross

Chantal Giraudeau was a princess—and she expected everyone to treat her royally. But special agent Caine O'Bannion wasn't about to indulge her every whim. His assignment was to guard her during her American tour. And protect her, he would...even if it meant keeping watch over her day and night!

The Adventurer
JAYNE ANN KRENTZ

Remember THE PIRATE (Temptation #287), the first book of
Jayne Ann Krentz's exciting trilogy Ladies and Legends? Next
month Jayne brings us another powerful romance, THE
ADVENTURER (Temptation #293), in which Kate, Sarah and
Margaret — three long-time friends featured in THE PIRATE
— meet again.

A contemporary version of a great romantic myth, THE
ADVENTURER tells of Sarah Fleetwood's search for long-
lost treasure and for love. Only when she meets her modern-
day knight-errant Gideon Trace will Sarah know she's found
the path to fortune and eternal bliss....

THE ADVENTURER — available in April 1990! And in June,
look for THE COWBOY (Temptation #302), the third book of
this enthralling trilogy.

In April, Harlequin brings you the
world's most popular romance author

JANET DAILEY

No Quarter Asked

Out of print since 1974!

After the tragic death of her father, Stacy's world is shattered. She
needs to get away by herself to sort things out. She leaves behind
her boyfriend, Carter Price, who wants to marry her. However, as
soon as she arrives at her rented cabin in Texas, Cord Harris, owner
of a large ranch, seems determined to get her to leave. When Stacy
has a fall and is injured, Cord reluctantly takes her to his own ranch.
Unknown to Stacy, Carter's father has written to Cord and asked
him to keep an eye on Stacy and try to convince her to return home.
After a few weeks there, in spite of Cord's hateful treatment that
involves her working as a ranch hand and the return of Lydia, his ex-
fiancée, by the time Carter comes to escort her back, Stacy knows
that she is in love with Cord and doesn't want to go.

Watch for *Fiesta San Antonio* in July and
For Bitter or Worse in September.

JDA-1

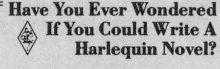

Have You Ever Wondered If You Could Write A Harlequin Novel?

Here's great news—Harlequin is offering a series of cassette tapes to help you do just that. Written by Harlequin editors, these tapes give practical advice on how to make your characters—and your story—come alive. There's a tape for each contemporary romance series Harlequin publishes.

Mail order only

All sales final

TO: **Harlequin Reader Service**
Audiocassette Tape Offer
P.O. Box 1396
Buffalo, NY   14269-1396

I enclose a check/money order payable to HARLEQUIN READER SERVICE® for $9.70 ($8.95 plus 75¢ postage and handling) for EACH tape ordered for the total sum of $_____*
Please send:

[ ] Romance and Presents   ☐ Intrigue
[ ] American Romance   ☐ Temptation
[ ] Superromance   ☐ All five tapes ($38.80 total)

Signature_____
                                                    (please print clearly)
Name:_____

Address:_____

State:_____ Zip:_____

*Iowa and New York residents add appropriate sales tax.   AUDIO-H

Harlequin Superromance®

LET THE GOOD TIMES ROLL . . .

Add some Cajun spice to liven up your New Year's celebrations and join Superromance for a romantic tour of the rich Acadian marshlands and the legendary Louisiana bayous.

CAJUN MELODIES, starting in January 1990, is a three-book tribute to the fun-loving people who've enriched America by introducing us to crawfish étouffé and gumbo, zydeco music and the Saturday night party, the *fais-dodo*. And learn about loving, Cajun-style, as you meet the tall, dark, handsome men who win their ladies' hearts with a beautiful, haunting melody....

Book One: *Julianne's Song*, January 1990
Book Two: *Catherine's Song*, February 1990
Book Three: *Jessica's Song*, March 1990